NATION OF THE MOON

Jonathan Byrd

Johnny Craft

Aaron Farrow

Cody Grady

John Graham

Patrick Handlon

Matthew Heslop

Casey Little

Christopher Moshier

E.M. Nelson

Marie Newbold

DEDICATION

This book is for every creative person who wanted to get their start in the publishing world. Your talent and hard work won't go unnoticed if you continue to persevere in your craft.

I also want to thank my family for their support of the time and energy it has taken me to chase this creative dream.

John Graham – FIGID Press

CONTENTS

STORIES AND AUTHORS

WE INTERRUPT THIS PROGRAM
By John Graham

6:28 PM Pacific Standard Time – June 22nd, 2024

We interrupt this program for a special report. WLFO 14 Los Angeles.

Reports are coming in from the East Coast about large scale animal attacks being experienced in multiple cities.

We are starting to get footage now, but it seems to be a wide scale situation where dogs are attacking those around them.

6:41 PM Pacific Standard Time

The following pictures were captured by our New York affiliate WGBS 8. It looks to be a large wolf. We will keep you updated as we wait for more pictures.

6:49 PM Pacific Standard Time

We are now receiving video from multiple sources that show people on the East Coast changing into wolf-like creatures and attacking those around them. These images are in the process of being verified.

7:15 PM Pacific Standard Time

The White House is unavailable for comment at this time. The Emergency Broadcast System has been activated on the East Coast.

7:41 PM Pacific Standard Time

We have on the line our Midwest correspondent, Chris Velikan, currently in Downtown Indianapolis at our affiliate location in the center of town. We are attempting to remotely access the cameras at this time. What can you tell us Chris?

Things are crazy here in Indy right now. The scenes are like a nightmare come to life, right out of a horror movie. I swear that I saw tourists on the square change into wolf-like creatures and then lunge out to attack those around them.

There are bodies on the streets outside the window. I'm in the sound booth now and not sure where the others are.

Chris, you say people have changed into wolves? Can you have someone else confirm this?

I can't find anyone else. I'm in the sound booth and don't see the newsman, Phil, in the studio any longer. Wait. Wait, I do see some movement by the desk.

Chris? Chris? Sorry folks, it looks like we've lost our connection with him. If you are just tuning in now, we are receiving video from all around the East and Midwest. It sounds crazy, but wolves are attacking people everywhere.

7:59 PM Pacific Standard Time

Folks, the following videos are extremely graphic, but are coming in unfiltered. Police are asking that you seek shelter immediately and avoid being in public unless absolutely necessary. I'm not sure what to say as we watch these clips. Oversized ferocious wolves attacking everyone they are near. I wouldn't believe this was happening if I wasn't watching the footage with you live.

8:25 PM Pacific Standard Time

Let's take a look at what folks are saying on social networks about this event.

@News6 I've just put my dogs outside.

@Whatahoax Is this a promo for a new werewolf movie?

@TrustinGod Gather in a church and pray. You will be saved.

@HappyMonkey My family is dead. Please help.

8:31 PM Pacific Standard Time

It's been just over two hours and we have confirmed a major incident throughout the Eastern and Midwestern states. More activity is being reported further west. We at WLFO commit to staying on the air and reporting to you during this crisis.

8:53 PM Pacific Standard Time

Reports have arrived from Utah where Temple Square has been overrun by wolves. The Las Vegas strip is in chaos at this time. We should have video in just a few minutes.

9:14 PM Pacific Standard Time

Folks, some of our technicians have left the studio to be with their families, but many of us are still committed to keeping you updated as events unfold.

9:27 PM Pacific Standard Time

More video coming in and it's…(cough)… disturbing. People are taking shelter and trying to reach…ugh…. loved ones. I'm sorry folks, but I've started feeling a bit sick. I'm..i'm.. here with you though until we understand what is happening. Speculation is rising about this being a biological attack. Please stay …..ughhh.

What's…what's.. happening to me? Argh.

Growwwl.

Awoooooo.

9:28 PM Pacific Standard Time

Beeeeeeeeeeeeeeeeeeeeep. Please Stand By.

IN THE HEN HOUSE
By Christopher Moshier

A picturesque view screams both peace and tranquility. The sun peaks through the tops of overgrown pines as it heads towards the horizon. It's time for her brilliance to be silent in this area of the globe, only to come yet again as the new dawn presents itself.

There are a diverse variety of birds chirping loudly. Perhaps they send greetings to the great fireball in the sky, thanking it for another day of allowing them to bask in its radiant preeminence.

"All through the night. I'll be awake, and I'll be with you. All through the night. This precious time when time is new..."

Cyndi Lauper's sweet, childlike voice permeates the immediate area with enough volume to be heard ever so slightly through the other sounds in the early evening air.

If you put the ear to the wind close enough, other sounds are also present. A monkey or two hooting. A lion's roar. A polar bear's growl. All brilliantly coordinated into the perfect ambient chorus.

Jacqueline Fernandez pushes her wheelbarrow, stocked with rake, broom, and shovel on top, headed towards the elephant cages. Armed with the tools of her trade, Jacqueline is prepared for the nightly duties that she both pleasantly and apprehensively looks forward to doing.

The zoo has been closed for about an hour now. The gate doors are locked. The last car has pulled away once that parent could get all the naughty kids inside. It was the blackmail of ice cream that did the trick. There is no more incredible bargaining chip than the promise of ice cream with chocolate sprinkles to an eight-year-old child.

The air is muggy as the remaining sun continues to beat down, persistent in continuing to be known at least for the remaining hour or so it has left until it rests below the horizon in preparation for returning about 6 am the following day.

The Seneca Park Zoo is a 20-acre wildlife park located in Rochester, New York. This menagerie is home to over 90 species of animals, including mammals, reptiles, birds, amphibians, fish, and arachnids. Its facility is illustriously accredited by the Association of Zoos and Aquariums, operated by the County of Monroe, with support from the Seneca Park Zoo Society.

It's a prime daily retreat for both the locals and visitors alike. For this modest-sized city, It's a tourist's economic solace from the grim and grime of their everyday lives. And for the weary parents, a perfect excuse to keep their children occupied while they breathe in some well-deserved Zen and grab a covert beer or two from the food court.

Jacqueline arrives at her intended destination, placing down the wheelbarrow handles and wiping off the sweat from her brow with the edge of her glove. The Elephant cages are about to get their sixth cleaning of the day. Not that she minds, but her only apprehensiveness in her job is cleaning the droppings from the present inhabitants.

In the containment area resides two of the planet's most beautiful creatures, Bela and Basil. Both harmoniously vocalize various greetings in the form of utterings and trumpeting's while flapping their ears and lifting their trunks to acknowledge Jacqueline's nightly arrival.

The duo has been at the zoo for about 35 years and is a couple of years older than that. They're both strong enough to push around cars and agile enough with their trunks to grab food or dab a brush from paint to canvas.

Criss-crossing her arms in front of her, Jacqueline waves as if she's attempting to flag down a Boeing 747. Jacqueline figures big animals, big motions. She'll even clap her hands a few times to spontaneously jumble up her greeting. Bela and Basil approve with their apparent giant smiles, or at least they look like giant smiles to her.

Jacqueline is originally from Culebra, an island municipality of Puerto Rico and part of the Spanish Virgin Islands. Natives to the island are known as Culebrenses.

Her father was a world-traveling journalist for National Geographic magazine. It was the paradise of Culebra where he met the woman he would marry, a young blogger before blogging was even considered a well-known practice. He became fascinated with this young woman and knew it was "love at first sight" if he was to believe in such a cliché.

Jacqueline's mother had a flair for mixing her travel writings with local politics. The municipal Socialist and Marxist legislators didn't always appreciate her ideals. But their governing platforms had become archaic, and they could also not deny progress if they wished to keep their jobs and get re-elected.

Consistently, Jacqueline's mother had a knack for getting herself in trouble with her written words and an equal aptitude for getting herself out of trouble with her spoken words. It was that grit and bravado that won over Jacqueline's Father's rigid heart.

Although fifteen years apart in age, they married and parented many children along their mostly untroubled nuptial journey. They had the typical disagreements a man and woman would have together in matrimony. Still, there was no infidelity, plenty of mutual respect, and a passionate fire that never fizzled.

Jacqueline is a product of both her parents with an adventurous spirit along with a wicked tongue and balls to the wall attitude to back it up.

It was the practice of her journalist parents that brought her to choose her impending career path. At present, Jacqueline is studying to be a veterinarian and zoologist so she can also travel the globe to help animals in duress and distress and document these travels giving eyes to the rest of the world's good and the bad towards the entire experience.

Jacqueline's spunk sometimes overshadows her actual abilities. She doesn't always know when to exercise her limits or restraint. When it comes to a brawl or the war of words, she sometimes lacks against her opponent, but that never stops her from going headfirst into a fight even when she is self-aware that she can't win. But she doesn't care. If it's with words or a fist, she'll take the bloody nose both figuratively and literally.

Bela and Basil weigh a combined 17,000 pounds. Their diet consists of lots of fruit, veggies, and bagels and no peanuts, by the way, as they contain way more protein than needed.

Elephants consume grasses, small plants, bushes, fruit, twigs, tree bark, and roots. Tree bark is a favorite food source for the mammoth creatures. It all contains calcium and roughage, which aids those massive tummies with digestion.

The two pachyderms consume up to 300 pounds of food each daily. About 30 pounds of that food comes back out in the form of poop that needs clean up. And they have no regard to where those 30 pounds end up. But the droppings are not as unpleasant as one would suspect, producing a musky smell, and is less offensive to one's nostrils than your average human public bathroom.

So, 600 pounds of food.

And 300 pounds of shit.

"Look at here. Always leaving me a fair bit of mess," Jacqueline calls out an octave higher than she would generally speak to make sure the Elephants can hear her. She'll pretend they can understand what she's telling them.

Amusing herself, Jacqueline walks up to the poop like the actor Jeff Goldblum did in the classic movie Jurassic Park. "That is one big pile of shit."

Making sure her gloves are on her hands snug and tight; Jacqueline goes ahead and kicks off her nightly ritual of raking and sweeping up the elephant dung into a manageable pile. She will dispense them in the dumpster appropriately labeled by Jacqueline using some left-over yellow paint. The dumpster reads - "B&B (Bela and Basil) Bombs.'"

A new song plays on the radio that Jacqueline grooves to as she goes about her poop duties.

"Intense silence as she walks into the room. Her black robes are trailing. Sister of the moon."

Fleetwood Mac belts out this classic with the intensity only Stevie Nicks can. She's a one-of-a-kind talent.

The same can be said for Jacqueline, who does her best to fit her lyrics with the song's tune. "If you're going to work with animals. It's a privilege to work with the animals. So, I don't mind picking up the poo. Now and again."

"If there is anything I can say about you, Jacqueline, it's your uncanny ability always to have a good and happy attitude." A different woman's voice is distinctly heard as she enters the containment area.

Aanya Bhrigu spares no time for official greetings and goes immediately to work conducting a visual assessment of the elephants. Her first order of business is to look for any abnormalities that may have happened throughout standard business hours.

"How can I mind this job?" Jacqueline flexes her right arm muscle showing fantastic definition. "I am turning into quite the specimen myself." And those muscles stem from lifting and cleaning up as much as 1,300 pounds of elephant dung a day, although she would prefer to do away with the smell that often clings to clothes which are mostly 20% elephant and 80% of her sweat.

But that's a small price to pay for the transformation that has begun to her figure. She especially doesn't mind because lately, Jacqueline's discovered the amount of muscle formed on her body. She particularly likes how her ass has been sitting in her jeans. Jacqueline never imagined such a perfect butt. To her amazement, superhero quality at best. Although she would have favored her breast cup didn't go down a size, she'll take the developed abs as compensation. All that Elephant shit picking up had indeed turned her physique into muscular perfection.

As far as what happens to all this shit when it's hauled away - a lot of it is used for composting. Most of it is gets turned into make paper. That's right - Elephant dung paper. It's not a new concept as it's been going on for decades.

A local gentleman implemented his business model considering the Zoos in Buffalo, Rochester, and Syracuse. With this entrepreneurial endeavor, his company manufactures unique, handcrafted, tree-free, eco-friendly, odorless (of course!) paper, gift and stationery products made exclusively from elephant poop, pooh, dung, turds, and stools. The whole gambit is soon to be followed by materials produced by donkeys, horses, and cows. That resource is plentiful in the meadows of Western New York.

It's turned into a highly profitable endeavor for this local native who is one of the few people that can gleefully handle all the shit you can throw at him. Although, he'd prefer to deliver by way of a tractor-trailer.

Jacqueline begins to shovel up the neat piles of poop. As incredible as you can shovel up poop, she dispenses the droppings into the motorized dumpster.

Aanya does her part by examining each elephant, looking for any cuts, scrapes, injuries, or illnesses that may have occurred throughout the zoo's business hours. This close examination is completed every twelve hours with other less thorough inspections throughout the day.

Aanya Bhrigu is originally from India. Most of Aanya's childhood years were spent in Bhuj, a municipality and the district headquarters of Kutch District in Gujarat.

Her father was a master craftsman with his embroidery work, one of legend. Philanthropists, statesmen (and women), celebrities, and elitists sought his work from all seven continents. Although he could work from his shop and live more a luxurious lifestyle than he did, he preferred to work off the land and practice his profession among the masses, constantly fine-tuning his craft in front of any spectators who found it of interest.

What pleased him the most and made him the most content was sharing his knowledge with others. Aanya's father would often turn down work to take his time on individual projects to teach others who wished to follow the same path.

The man had lived a harsh and tired existence with multiple tragedies that affected his psyche greatly. It gave him a distinctive perspective about life that money was essential to survive, but it wasn't what made him rise from his bed daily.

Aanya's mother had similar sensibilities. She was a traditionalist but also walked a fine line between heritage and the equality of her gender. Much of her younger years were spent traveling the world with her parents spending a great deal of time in the United States.

There was a desire to see equal pay and comparable representation for the women in her country. She was also quick to point out that the broken family in the US has caused various social issues. She didn't want the same thing to happen in her country.

Aanya also had two younger sisters. Unfortunately, and tragically, at the age of fourteen, Aanya lost her entire family in the 2001 earthquake. The Bhuj earthquake of 2001 was a massive catastrophe that occurred on January 26th, 2001, in the Indian state of Gujarat, on the Pakistani border.

The quake occurred while the entire country was celebrating Republic Day, a national holiday where the nation marked the date on which the constitution of India came into effect. A bitter-sweet observance interrupted by the forces of nature that took the lives of twenty-thousand people.

Aanya became an orphan of her village that day along with dozens of other children. As the town began to rebuild, these parentless children would take turns staying among family members and friends who now had found themselves impoverished. It made for an uneasy situation as many of these adolescents were exploited by people with more than noble objectives.

Due to her father's wealth, Aanya found she was better off than most. Because of her parent's estate, she could take advantage of the money by furthering her education. When she came of age, she turned over the remainder of her father's holdings to the children still living in the slums of the village.

Women and girls are particularly disadvantaged there. A large number of those living in poverty are female-headed households. Girls had to often drop out of school at a very early age and are therefore unable to secure a good education which would've allowed them to break out of the cycle of poverty as they grew older.

With her father's inheritance that she'd left behind, Aanya hoped the pattern of poverty could be averted. And from the communications she receives from friends remaining in India, there is good news on that these days. Due to her funds and current technology, homeschooling became the new normal in her village, allowing females to take care of the household while getting a solid education base.

Aanya was very much like her father having little interest in money and more interest in self-fulfillment. There was the personification of a fighter through her early teen years that grew with intensity into adulthood. As a child, one of Aanya's idols was a prominent woman named Seema Rao, who she idolized with the highest of regard.

Seema Rao was the first Indian woman commando trainer. She's trained soldiers in India for over two decades. She is an expert in close-quarter battle — the art of fighting in tight proximity — and training various Indian special forces.

Seema's story touched Aanya as they were both victims of sexual harassment in their youth. A situation neither of them was going to be unprepared for again. It's what fired up Aanya's tenacity at such an early age.

And just like Seema, Aanya joined the Indian military. Even though today it is against country policy for women to fight in combat, it was never her intention to fight when she enlisted. But there were unwritten rules, and skirmishes presented little choice than for Aanya to defend herself. These skirmishes would only be a legend, never to be reported in any official capacity.

In the service, Aanya achieved a black belt in Taekwondo and Krav Maga and a 5th-degree black belt in military martial arts. In theory, being passive was a utopian state of mind, but Aanya wasn't against knocking someone on their ass if they truly deserved it.

Along with her military training, she also became an excellent medic. Aanya found her empathy regarding animals most certainly outweighed any sympathy towards human beings. In caring for injured animals used by the military, she discovered her true love in zoology.

Once her military service was complete, Aanya enrolled in zoology courses conducted at the Miranda House College in New Delhi. Upon her completion, she jumped at the chance to come to the United States and study and has been at the Seneca Park Zoo ever since and loving every minute of it.

Each evening, Aanya conducts a visual assessment of the elephants. From the tip of the trunk to the tail and everything in between is scrutinized. On cue, the elephants will present different body parts so they can be observed closely.

Aanya uses operant conditioning and positive reinforcement to teach the elephants the behaviors needed for a more cooperative examination. Each elephant has the choice to participate or not. Nothing is forced.

When Bela and Basil participate, Aanya rewards them with their favorite foods and says "good job" to affirm that behavior. Some days, an elephant may not feel like participating in training, and that's perfectly acceptable. Just like human beings, Elephants have their good and bad days as well.

Aanya's number one concern is to make sure the elephants can trust her. There must be a positive view of their guardian and these training sessions, so she never forces them to do anything they don't want to do. Rewarding good behaviors while respecting their choice to participate has helped build the unequivocal trust they now have.

As soon as Aanya has completed her assessment, she and Jacqueline provide the elephants with fresh hay and water for their consumption.

While the elephants enjoy their evening snack in the containment area, both Aanya and Jacqueline go about cleaning their outdoor habitats and freshen up the enrichment feeders. Their daily maintenance of the Bela and Basil's habitat includes cleaning the pools, refilling divots the animals have made in the ground, and creating large mounds of dirt and sand.

The elephants enjoy going for a swim—especially on hot summer days—and will often roll around the mounds, lean up against them for a rest, and toss the dirt and sand onto their backs to protect their skin from the sun.

Once everything is clean and tidy to the elephant's liking, Jacqueline calls Bela and Basil into what she calls the "school" to conduct training sessions. In this area, puzzle feeders and other large toys are set up to encourage the elephants to explore, forage and play.

It's just another area in the structure that's solely in use for coaching. Mostly, it's just an excuse for all four, humans and elephants alike, to get together and bond, throwing or punting a colossal ball around.

Creedence Clearwater Revival eggs them on with a punchy melody that will only become ironic an hour or so from now.

"I see the bad moon arising. I see trouble on the way. I see earthquakes and lightnin'. I see bad times today."

The job is relatively simple once the habitat is clean. Jacqueline and Aanya spend the second part of their time focusing on husbandry, enrichment, and training to provide the best quality care for Bela and Basil.

Foot care is a vital element of elephant health, so Aanya routinely inspects their cuticles, nails, and pads (soles) and trim them to prevent cracks.

As Aanya tends to that need, Jacqueline hangs out resting on a big pile of hay. "I hope we make them happy. It would break my heart if I knew they weren't."

"The decision to bring them here was made long before we ever arrived. Christ. Before you were even born." Aanya always speaks as if she's giving out every ounce of wisdom available to her. There's a self-induced internal pressure always to have an answer for everything and the feeling of inadequacy if she doesn't.

"I do realize that nothing we do is going to allow them to thrive," Jacqueline sits up, crossing her legs. "I do realize we're here to make their lives as meaningful and as comfortable as possible. This shouldn't be it. They shouldn't have to die here. They're adaptive to herds as dogs are to pacts. It's an injustice for them not to live as nature intended."

Aanya motions to Bela to put her left foot down off the oversized stool and replace it with the right foot. "You sound like a child, Jack."

Jacqueline shoots Aanya a quick grin and points her finger towards her, "I knew you were going to say something like that. And then you're going to tell me life is a massive injustice or something around that line of thinking and then finish it up with some story that contradicts the original narrative assuring hope and stability in the world."

"That's why the realization that no matter how much we love elephants and want to be near elephants and see elephants, the decision is that it was fundamentally wrong for us to do this. Captivity in the United States for these magnificent creatures will soon only be in BLOGs and VLOGs. People will have to go see the elephants as they were intended rather than the peak at them through an enclosure."

"And then our jobs will move to the wild where I want to be anyways," Jacqueline states with cheerful optimism. "We'll be knee-deep in action."

Aanya has seen her fair share of action through the years, and that adage 'Careful what you wish for' pops in her head. "Alright there,

Seema Rao, Warrior Princess," she teasingly calls out Jacqueline with an obscure allusion to an Indian legend not many outsiders would get.

Jacqueline doesn't follow the reference, "Who is Seema Rao?"

"India's Wonder Woman. Like Diana Prince, but Seema Rao." And now Aanya doesn't even think Jack gets the Diana Prince reference; the alter ego of the comic book character. Instead of confusing Jacqueline further, Aanya attempts to explain, "She is known to be India's first woman commando trainer. She's trained Special Forces of India for over two decades. She is, without a doubt, my idle."

"And this is a real person?"

"Yes. Seema Rao is a genuine person."

"Have you ever met her?"

"Never face to face. I did see Seema speak while I was at the military academy in Dehradun. She can be very inspiring. She's a big part of who I turned out to be."

This piques Jacqueline's curiosity as she fancies herself a badass in the ways of the world yet, in the reality of it all, hasn't had any experience to back that up, "Have you ever killed anyone?"

This question doesn't affect Aanya in the least. It's a fair question aimed at a soldier, "Women aren't allowed in combat in India."

You would think that this would be the end of that question, but not for Jacqueline, "That's not what I asked."

Aanya is tending to Basil, now scrubbing down one of his legs with lukewarm water, "There are ways around anything, Jack. There are rules towards belief and tradition, and statehood. But when a situation presents itself, all that is superseded by objection and survival."

Jacqueline takes that as a very diplomatic way as saying 'yes' to her question. "I could never kill anything," she just wanted that to be known. "That's why I work here. So, I can nurture the living. Make the lives of these magnificent creatures all that much better."

Aanya delivers a big smile when hearing this. She is in total agreement as she looks up towards Basil, "It's just like my large friend here. Gentle as a sweet summer breeze. But cross him. Do something to piss him off. He'll take you out."

Bela and Basil have finished their pampering for the day. The young women bring the elephants back to their holding area for socialization. All four of them hang out, watching the moon begin to peak from the clouds. The sun has almost totally disappeared now. There's a clock hanging outside the containment that reads 8:15 pm.

Aanya follows up on their previous conversation with an inquiry of her own, "I thought you were passive?"

Jacqueline is taken back by this question as if it was an attack on her morality, "I am extremely passive."

"Passive-aggressive perhaps," Aanya giggles as she takes a swig of water from her water jug. "You can't be passive and then get into fights all the time. And why do you go to those places when your end goal is just to get your ass kicked?"

Aanya is referencing that Jacqueline has a habit of getting all dressed up in full makeup and donning high heels. She intends to go out for a night to any local watering hole just looking for an excuse for some other bitch, as she would call them, to look at her sideways. Jacqueline will purposely flirt with men who are clearly with other women. She would do mostly anything to test someone else's resolve.

"My end goal is never to get my ass kicked," Jacqueline attempts to defend her occasional careless actions. "My end goal is the talk myself out of getting my ass kicked."

Aanya is almost at full chortling mode, "Is that what that is?"

Jacqueline pleads her defense to her jury of one, "I grew up with a parent who was a master of talking herself out of anything. No matter how much I've tried my entire life, I've been unable to master that skill. And passive-aggressive is acting indirectly aggressive. I'm not an angry person. I want to be more assertive aggressive. I would think more of an aggressive passive. Because if I'm simply going to be passive, I'm not going to change anything in the world. If I'm aggressive, then I'm just a bully. But if I am aggressive passive, then I can stand up to a bully while talking them down at the same time."

Aanya is amazed at the amount of thought put into that last statement and even more surprised at how agreeable she is to it. She switches conversation gears, "Then why do you want me to teach you all these fighting moves if your weapon of choice is going to be belligerent diplomacy?"

"Because you remind me of my mother."

Aanya almost spits out her water. She looks directly at Jack, making sure she is aware of the blatant rolling of her eyes.

"I mean. You are what I aspire to be in a socialized sense. You are gentle yet tough. Your words are authoritative, yet you say them with such elegance."

"Because that's who I've been conditioned to be my entire life, Jack. It's not something you learn. It's who you are. You can't be me anymore than I can be you."

"But I can be as close as possible. I mean, seriously. What do you see when you look at me?"

"You're a kind, compassionate girl, Jack. I wish I could be more like you. What is the American phrase? Is the grass always greener? But I don't want you to be something that you're not. I want you to be that sweet, sympathetic, empathic girl. The world certainly needs more like you and less like me. Violence is easy. Equanimity takes skill."

As if there was some fate or devilish plot involved this evening, the voice of Billy Squier began to belt out of the radio.

"Lonely is the night. When you find yourself alone. Your demons come to light. And your mind is not your own. Lonely is the night. When there's no one left to call. You feel the time is right. Say the writing's on the wall."

No other words are fitting for what's about the come.
The clock turns 8:25 pm.
The sun is gone.

The moonlight hits Aanya's eyes at the perfect angle. They begin to glow a blazing red.

Jacqueline and Aanya stare at each other for a solitary moment giving each other a nonverbal validation that something unnatural was occurring.

Aanya's head launches into a series of twitches as her teeth go about lengthening past her jaw. Her hands expand outright, with dark hairs beginning to protrude through the pours. There is almost a semblance of a scream from Aanya towards what is occurring. The awkward screech is very similar to a subtle growl.

In the deep night air echoing throughout the landscape, dozens if not hundreds of howls can be heard. The culmination of yowls, yelps, and barks merge in a bellowing chorus, reaching a magnitude of crescendo. Then a split second, it was gone fading ever so quickly into oblivion.

When this night is over, it will be documented that the moon glowed more brightly this evening than can previously be recalled.

Standing where Aanya had once stood, crouched down on all fours, materializes a drooling, growling hairy beast with sharp teeth protruding through the gumline. The creature sheds off its shirt revealing its breasts also covered with hair.

Jacqueline and the creature (that had once been Aanya) gaze at each other for several moments. Both attempt to surmise and consider the other's move.

Jacqueline's initial scare had dissipated into a dangerous curiosity. Her wonderment held any scared that she might have initially had at bay.

There was not a choice. It was a call of nature. It was instinctual. The creature lashes forward.

Very fast and very agile, Jacqueline rolls herself backward and flips to her feet using her arms.

The creature lunges towards Jacqueline.

Jacqueline grabs the broom that had been resting on the wall. She fends off the creature's bite by blocking it with the handle she now has in hand and shoving it into the creature's mouth—the broom snaps in two.

While the wolf-like creature spits out the disgust of the taste of wood chunks from its mouth, Jacqueline picks up a rake and hits the beast in the back, so the forks puncture the creature's skin.

The beast screams out in pain. Jacqueline has managed to enrage the beast further and increase the viciousness of its attack.

The werewolf advances on Jack, flailing its sharp claws frantically in no set pattern.

Jacqueline is at a loss on how to defend herself from this attack. She sprints as fast as she can towards the beast, drops to the ground, and slides across the floor like a rag doll. As she skims underneath the beast's legs, she is cut twice by those serrated claws.

As the creature composes itself from the pain and refocuses, a winded Jacqueline limply lifts herself from the ground to her feet. Blood now drips from her forearm. Fortunately, these are only superficial wounds. She runs towards the exit gates that house the Elephants in an attempt to block any further attack.

But just as the gate is going to close, the creature jumps, sticking its arm and leg in places that prevent it from sealing shut completely. Jacqueline frantically opens and closes the gate door producing enough force to slam it into the beast's body, causing irritating trauma. After enough blows to the point of excruciating pain, the werewolf concedes and lets Jacqueline go and allows the door to be closed.

Securing the gate door, Jacqueline shouts out, "Shit," after realizing what she's just done. The werewolf is now locked in with Bela and Basil.

The werewolf turns its attention from Jack and towards the two mammoth pachyderms.

Jacqueline screams out in panic, "DON'T YOU HURT THEM!" She frantically unlatches the gate door kicking it wide open. "Get your hairy, growling ass out here!"

The werewolf is more than happy to comply. This thing looks at

Jacqueline dead in the eyes as it displays its sharp teeth, looking almost like it's grinning. With strong paws, front and center, the creature lunge once again towards Jacqueline.

There's an attempt to leap out of the way, but Jacqueline isn't quick enough and gets the brunt of a claw that rips into her left arms intense this time. If Jacqueline had waited for half a second longer to leap out of the way, her arms would no longer be attached to her body. The blood spurts to the ground and surrounding wall. Cries of agony are tumultuous, hitting all the four-square corners of the zoo. All the animals react with their cries of concern and fear.

Jacqueline Fernandez needs to think quickly. She could no longer concern herself with both protecting the Elephants and the creature that was once her friend. She would have to accept that person doesn't exist anymore. Her primary duty from the first day of obtaining the job at the zoo was to take care and protect these animals. It was all or nothing. There were no more choices. No more traps to bait this creature into were apparent—no more options to consider. Jacqueline came to the painful decision that this creature has to die.

All those muscles from weeks of cleaning up elephant dung have paid off in the most obscure of ways. Jacqueline's hamstrings and quadriceps, along with the pure adrenaline shooting through the body, made any running look like superhuman speed. She is fast.

Chasing right behind her is the creature determined to make Jacqueline its primary victim this night.

There is a security office at the edge of the zoo that contains sedatives and tranquilizers. And although Jacqueline's never seen it with those beautiful brown eyes, there's the knowledge of a gun that the emergency response team has stored there. To her understanding, it has never been used until now. If there were a punchline, if this were a joke, it would be that Aanya is on the emergency response team, with the funniest part being that the keys to her demise are now sitting in her back pocket or its back pocket.

What came first, the chicken or the egg? Jacqueline needs those keys to take the creature down, but the beast needs to be stopped to get those keys.

As Jacqueline runs at top speed with the beast in direct pursuit, she forms a plan. Her arm is also gushing blood. She needs to tend to that before she passes out.

Dashing past the food court, a flicker of an idea came to Jacqueline. She leaps onto one of the picnic tables in the courtyard and then jumps to another table and then another until reaching one of the concessions.

If there was a time to do something stupid, this was it as she pushes her feet full force off of the edge of a table. In midair, the entire weight of her body heads towards the takeout window. Jacqueline lifts both arms over her face to protect her head as she deliberately goes crashing through the flimsy barrier that is supposed to keep unwanted individuals out of the structure.

Inside the concession stand, Jacqueline takes a quick inventory of her surroundings, looking for something to give her an advantage. From the corner of her eye, a reflection of herself is visible. It's a giant silver commercial refrigerator. For the second time today, the movie Jurassic Park enters her mind. Could this possibly work?

Jacqueline unlatches the hook from the front door of the concession stand and cracks open the door about two inches. Crying out with a series of loud yelps, she hopes it's enough for the werewolf to hear it and head her way. It works.

As the werewolf crashes through the door to the food stand, it looks at the refrigerator seeing Jacqueline's reflection. The creature runs towards the fridge without a thought, crashing into the appliance full-force, making a magnificent dent.

As it shakes off the throbbing impact, the werewolf tries to catch its breath and regain its faculties. That's the opening Jacqueline needs to have enough time to put her hand into the creature's back pocket and pulls out the keys that will fulfill her plan.

Darting back towards the concession stand window, she leaps through the opening to the outside, dropping headfirst towards the ground, rolling herself out of the full impact by maneuvering her shoulder to hit first, recovering to her feet, and running off without even the slightest of error in that entire maneuver.

Sprinting at full speed, she heads towards the emergency area.

The werewolf continues the pursuit once all its senses return.

With the stamina, tenacity, and stubbornness of what makes a world-class runner, Jacqueline succeeds in making it to the protective service building with moments to spare to accomplish her mission. There is no time to catch a breath. There is no time to fumble through the keys. There is no time to contemplate her bleeding wounds. There is no time to think about her impending doom.

And she doesn't. Jacqueline focuses on her objective. The door is unlocked and then locked again behind her. She pulls guns and ammunition from the lockers. She grabs a couple of cans of pepper spray off the shelving.

Kicking open the door to the service building, Jacqueline is armed and ready with the tranquilizer rifle slung over one arm and two cans of pepper spray in either hand. She knows she'll have to hinder the creature before she can get a clear shot. She's no sharpshooter.

The werewolf is at its full speed, running right at Jacqueline like a derailed train devoid of its tracks. There was no time for it to stop to access the situation. Pure animal instinct was driving this primordial engine.

Jacqueline flipped off the tops of the pepper spray with each thumb and pushed down with her index fingers. The werewolf runs into the mist, ingesting a healthy dose of the contents in the mouth and eyes.

Jacqueline falls to the ground. From this position, she can snatch the rifle's strap off her shoulder. Grasping the gun with both hands, she aims it at the creature, who is making another leap towards her. The beast is now blinded and in coercion but can still hear and smell his prey.

The gun is fired. The dart tipped with a hypodermic needle embeds itself into the werewolf's flesh.

Jacqueline rolls herself out of the impending attack recovering herself to her knee. She aims the gun again and fires it five more times, hoping and praying this isn't going to kill her attacker, who at this point doesn't seem to be phased by being shot.

There's the yearning of just incapacitating the creature with the hope that somehow something of Aanya survives in there.

It lashes at her again, and she rolls on the rocky ground to evade this attack cutting herself on some of the smaller, sharper stones.

Jacqueline stands gashed up from head to toe, her clothes filthy from the Earth. Her breathing is difficult as she gasps for the fresh night air. But she can rest easy now or at least easier. The sedative in the creature's body is taking effect now. The beast is slowing. Groggy. Stupefied. It drops to the ground, unconscious.

With her remaining strength, Jacqueline drags the werewolf across the zoo grounds and gently places it into an empty cage, ensuring it's triple locked. The creature is panting very shallow now.

Jacqueline turns her attention towards herself, grabbing gauze and disinfectants from one of the medical kits found all over the facility. Carrying the box labeled "first aid," she drops to the ground just a few feet from the cage.

In all the running and jumping and chasing, she didn't realize how much she was hurt. It also became apparent that every muscle in her body is now screaming out in pain. And on top of all that, there was unprecedented exhaustion.

With all the energy she had left, she started patching herself together.

You can hear Dave "Doc" Robinson and King Harvest over the park's sound system.

"Dancing in the moonlight. Everybody's feeling warm and bright. It's such a fine and natural sight. Everybody's dancing in the moonlight."

Jacqueline laughs as she reviews in her head all the music that's been playing during her shift. It's as if this night was all preordained. Is such a thing possible? Was this orchestrated? Was this night constructed to play out the way it did? And who the hell made all the music selections?

Then she remembered. It's June 22nd. It was the evening of the Strawberry Moon. The Full Moon. The celestial phenomenon occurs when the moon is at the closest point to Earth in its orbit. Earth's only satellite appears larger and brighter than a typical full moon.

Legend says the full moon brings out all the crazies. If she remembers correctly, it has something to do with tides being higher because the gravity from the moon and sun are pulling together on the Earth. She may never know how that coordinates with what happened this evening, but there is undoubtedly one thing for sure. She's glad it's over. At least for now.

****

Jacqueline's eyes slowly appear from behind her lids that seem to be stuck by her dry, crusty lacrimal fluid or what people would call tears. Light is apparent even with her eyes closed. She guesses it must be daytime. And there it is. Now that her eyes are fully open, there is the sun front and center.

Moans from the cage in front of her are ones from Aanya. She's not in any better shape than Jacqueline is. Aanya manages to do a quick inventory of herself and then looks toward Jacqueline with an emotion that's rarely seen from her; fear.

Jacqueline goes into one of the storage areas pulling out one of the elephant's neutral-colored blankets in anticipation of putting it over Aanya's half-naked body once her transformation back to her original self has completed.

Jacqueline hugs her tightly as Aanya shakes uncontrollably. "You're ok. You're ok," Jacqueline does her best to try to calm her friend.

"Jack? What in the hell did I do?"

Jacqueline looks at her friend with no answer.

Aanya is a tactician and a soldier. She's starting to put the pieces together. Another primary concern enters her thoughts. She cries out, "Bela! Basil! What did I do to them?" All this fresh in her mind, Aanya's tears begin to flow by the sheer terror of what could have happened to the elephants.

"No," insists Jacqueline. "No," she insists again, shaking her friend. "Look at me."

In hysterics, Aanya can hardly catch her breath.

Jacqueline tries again, this time shaking her harder, "Look at me. Bela and Basil are fine. They aren't harmed. Not even one cubicle on those giant feet of theirs."

Aanya looks deep into Jack's eyes. She searches for a lie or a deception. There wasn't one to find.

Jacqueline helps Aanya out of the cage and to her feet. "Come on. Let's go see them."

Both women enter the elephant's containment area.

With a sense of the danger now past, Bela and Basil build the courage to move forward to make sure Aanya is who she is typically. In whatever manner these animals process events and information in their mammal minds, they had some understanding of what had transpired this night. Perhaps just as much knowledge as Jacqueline has.

"What in the hell was that?" Aanya looks all-around at the mess.

"What do you remember?" Jacqueline is fascinated in knowing if Aanya can recall anything that had transpired in the out-of-the-ordinary early morning hours.

"All I know is I had a deep craving for flesh. Fresh meat. And that has faded along with everything like waking from a bad dream."

"That's not a classic horror cliché at all." Jacqueline attempts some type of humor towards all this.

Aanya attempts to join her, "I guess the cliché had to come from somewhere."

"It was literarily a horror movie," Jacqueline tries to comprehend her own words at the same time as trying to have them make sense to Aanya as she rattles them off. "There was a full moon. You turned into a werewolf. We struggled. I was able to apprehend you. None of the animals were hurt. We may need a hospital."

Aanya has yet another thought, "What time is it?"

Both at the same time, they look at the clock hung on the wall. It's telling them it's 9 am.

Jacqueline states the obvious, "I guess we missed today's opening. But I guess that's alright because there is no staff and there are no visitors."

"Just us," Aanya iterates a half dozen times.

Jacqueline now asks the question of all questions, "What if it happens again?"

Aanya grabs Jacqueline by the arm and leads her into the park.

From storage, Aanya pulls out a shock collar, "All progressive zoos and wild animal parks use management and positive reinforcement ONLY even with large and potentially dangerous animals, but they didn't always."

"I didn't even know this building existed." Jacqueline pokes around this shack that sits at the edge of the zoo. She always thought it was just that, an old, abandoned shed. Looks were very much deceiving as it looks as if the inside had been reinforced and painted recently.

"And either does anyone else. Just myself and the zoo director," Aanya explains. "It was all to be cataloged and sent to some kind of museum. Lucky for us, it never made it that far."

Aanya goes about tooling a makeshift collar and puts it around her neck to make sure it fits.

"Now," Aanya begins to explain to Jack, "when the sun is ready to set, I will put this on."

Aanya hands a reluctant Jacqueline the controller. "If I make any aggressive moves towards anyone or anything, you shock the shit out of me."

The next thing Aanya does is pick up the shotgun, loads it, and purposely cocks it for dramatic effect. "And if that doesn't stop me, this will."

"But what if it goes in reverse next time. What if I turn, and you're left fending me off?"

Well, shit! That was an excellent point, Aanya unwillingly concedes. She goes ahead and pulls out a second shock collar putting it around Jacqueline's neck to make sure that it also fits, and attaches the controller for that one to her belt.

"What if we both turn?"

Jacqueline infers Aanya with her questions, but she doesn't lash out because Aanya knows they're excellent questions. "I don't know. We'll figure it out as we go."

Their next stop is to the food court, where they store up reserves for the day, grabbing water and snacks. They decide to walk into the city to see if what happened to them took place elsewhere.

Jacqueline and Aanya have a long discussion about leaving the animals, but they couldn't explore solo. The unknown was too dangerous at this point. It's unanimously decided between the two that they travel at least three or four miles in any direction and assess the situation. Then they would have to determine their next movie, but they would do it strategically and cautiously.

Both ensure that Bela, Basil, and the rest of the animals are settled and have provisions for the day. When they were satisfied that all would be alright for the time being, they began their walk towards the city, walking away from the zoo.

Aanya takes a deep look into Jacqueline's eyes. "I'm going to teach you how to fight."

"That is probably a good idea," Jacqueline agrees.   THE END

CASTAWAY
By Marie Newbold

The boy broke through the brambles before Karen did, holding aside the thorniest branches to protect her. She clasped the hand he held out to help over roots and debris, keeping a firm grip on the shotgun in her other hand, as the two did their best to step out onto the sidewalk noiselessly. When her orthotic shoes were finally steady on the sidewalk, Karen turned to look over her shoulder.

The house was fully on fire now. Flames were visible in the bedroom that Karen had slept ever since she and her husband had returned from their honeymoon. The heat swept through her home, explosions and crackling covered any sounds she was making, a block away. Karen pressed her lips together and silently said her goodbyes. Goodbye to her grandmother's porcelain dinnerware, painted with violets; goodbye to quilts handmade for her bed; goodbye to the letters from her father when he was away in the war.

Goodbye to the wedding album, the only place left she could see Frank's face, the husband she had married before thirty and lost after seventy.

Karen turned her head, white hair greyed by ash, soot, and dirt from the bramble patch, to the boy next to her. Tears had cleared streaks through the grime on his cheeks. The side of his head towards her no longer had any hair – escaping the fire had exacted that small price from his mane of dirty blond hair. She swallowed a few times, trying to find her old schoolmarm voice. "Come on Tyler. There's nothing more to be done here, and we need to get to someplace safe."

Tyler turned his head. "Ms. Mercer, don't you think you've paid enough? You should take care of yourself. I'll figure out something."

Karen snorted. Some things didn't change no matter how much

the world was falling apart. The bravado of a boy on the cusp of manhood always made an appearance. She tucked the shotgun under her right arm, then fed her left arm through Tyler's elbow. "I need your young eyes to help me see the way, dear. I don't think I'll make it without you." Pull, pull. "When we get where we're going, I'm going to need your help getting in. The key was in my house and is probably a melted lump now. "This time, when she pulled, Tyler's steps followed. "I helped her shut up the house myself, so I know she took all the sheets off the bed and emptied everything out of the fridge. The way things are now, we'll need to work hard to get breakfast tomorrow."

Tyler swiped his cheeks, smearing ash and tears in mask across his cheekbones. "I'm so sorry they burned your home."

Karen felt a thundering storm of emotions at the thought of her losses. She nodded to Tyler and to her internal whirlwind. "Well, I'm not exactly happy about it either. I could be helplessly devastated by the loss of all my things and leave you to run off and lick my wounds." She chuckled, a dry, raspy sound from a very old throat. "But, my dear boy, I'm an old woman. Before I lost the things in my house, I've lost my husband, my sister, my parents, and a rather large number of lovely cats. You don't live for seven decades without learning to deal with loss. So I don't think I'll do that today, if you've no objection."

They walked for half an hour before she spoke again. "Tyler, dear, in this situation you need to learn the ways of the soldier. We can't focus on the sadness, but we do need to focus on that rage."

The steady steps lost their rhythm, the shaggy head shook its half a head of hair. "What?"

Pulling his arm to keep him moving, Karen looked off into the distance and continued. "Frank told me that it was the only way to survive the war - to get mad enough to commit violence. If we want to live through this next week, we're going to have to stay angry enough to fight for the right, apparently." Karen hiked the shotgun up where it was drooping again. "Think about it. We'll discuss it later."

The old woman and the young man continued walking for hours. Karen was a strong-willed woman, but seven decades had robbed her of any hope of endurance in power walking from one end of the city to the other. She had to stop for frequent breaks, and they had to choose their path very carefully. Not only did they have to avoid the well-traveled roads where Austin's posse would run them to ground and complete the lynching they had set out to do, but Tyler also hadn't managed to grab shoes. Without a flashlight, without streetlamps, and in the light of the three-quarter moon, they had to check carefully to make sure Tyler wouldn't be treading over broken glass or sharp metal debris.

They couldn't be completely quiet, stumbling as they were. Eventually, Karen couldn't quite keep from grumbling irritated observations. "This should be fifteen-minute drive, not a six-hour walk," she said as she passed the halfway mark. "Betcha Deputy Bob has taken everyone's statements and is sitting around with a coffee cup by now," she said as they navigated an alleyway behind a Starbucks.

"How in the name of Zeus is this helping anybody?" she exclaimed as they watched a corner market go up in flames as well. Tyler shook his head, jaw clenched at the sight of a young woman wearing a University of Kentucky sweatshirt trussed up on the sidewalk across the way. More of the "Missouri Civilian Defense Association" members could be seen around the lot. The pair quickly ducked out of sight and continued on their way. There was nothing they could do to help now, only do their best to survive the night themselves.

It took seven hours to complete the journey that they had begun due to the fire. Through careful planning, they had managed to meet no one else that entire time. Ducking any sounds of people awake, creeping through back alleys and resting against trash cans, they endured. They had left the denser parts of the city behind to walk down a country gravel road. Gates were closed on many of the long driveways leading back to rambling farmhouses. Many of the homes had parked vehicles, undoubtedly empty of fuel and therefore nothing but rolling barricades now, across driveways. A few homes, often the newer-built homes of the recently affluent, were burned shells empty of the families that had been planning for the upcoming Fourth of July a month ago. Karen stumbled to a halt at a dirt lane cut in an overgrown hedge. "Here we are."

The two forced themselves down the little dirt lane. Neither had the energy to lift their kicked up a small dust cloud. Tyler walked on the higher ground in the middle where grass blocked the sharp edges of the rocks from his battered bare feet. Karen chose the right rut and struggled to not fall on the uneven path. Dreading another burnt shell, Karen almost fainted with relief when the small yellow plaster home proved to be intact. There was no need for a key, true, as the door swung loose on its frame and many of the windows were broken. But the living room within still held the worn floral sofa and the rug hand woven from old t-shirts. Karen muttered a silent thank you to her friend, gone to protect her grandsons.

"Ms Mercer, are you sure we're welcome here?" Tyler's voice was rough and scratchy.

"Of course we are, dear. I helped my friend make that rug on the floor ten years ago. She's a bit odd, so she doesn't have anything fancy around here. No luxuries to be jealous of, though I think we'll find a few hidden gems to keep us for the next week. Then the world will shift again, I'm sure." She lay down on the couch, as she had so many time before. "This is where I sleep when I stay here. Why don't you go find us some water, and then you can rest in Helen's bed?" Cradling the shotgun, Karen began working her shoes loose.

She had enough energy to murmur her thanks for the glass of water Tyler had pressed into her hand and to pull the quilt over her. With one hand on the shotgun, she went to sleep.

*　*　*

"Thank you for being here, Ladies and Gentleman, let's get started." The mayor's press secretary was at the podium. Deputy Bob, a veteran of the city police with 20 years of experience, was sitting in for the Sheriff. It was one of the many duties that the Deputy performed that cemented his position as the next Sheriff, once old Andrew retired.

The room quieted. "As you all know, tonight is the full moon we've been dreading after last month's events. Following directives from the governor's office, we will be doing a final roundup of all known out-of-state visitors for detention in prepared holding cells this evening to prevent any wolf infection damage in the State of Missouri. Anyone from out of state who wishes to assure the safety of the citizens of Missouri is encouraged to report to the Sheriff's office or to the hospital to check into a facility for observation. Any such person can be assured of being treated with the highest respect during this difficult time.

"Questions."

Deputy Bob scanned the few reporters who had attended today's press conference. There weren't many – with the state not getting any imports of coal from across the state line, there wasn't power for recharging batteries for TV cameras and the like. Old-style paper reporters and some radio reporters were still in action, though. Bob wasn't surprised when Wright Canton stood up, but he did manage to refrain from groaning out loud. "Mrs. Secretary, could you please tell me what has happened to those citizens who have been apprehended by the self-styled Missouri Civilian Defense Association, and what steps are being taken to de-legitimize this terrorist group after their multiple acts of arson in the last week?"

The press secretary's voice went flatter than the local farming fields. "The Missouri Civilian Defense Association was officially deputized by the governor's office two weeks ago, sir. We have lodged multiple complaints with the state administration of this organization regarding the unfortunate handling of Miss Herring and the damage to the Casey's at Jackson and 3rd last week. Miss Herring has been returned to her family.

"The governor's office has not responded to our complaints in this matter. Their recommendation for tonight is to work in cooperation with the MCDA during tonight's potentially dangerous natural events. Next."

No one else cared to air the dirty laundry that was Austin Striefer's Missouri Civilian Defense Association that day. The press conference continued, listing the details of tonight's precautions and emergency numbers. Deputy Bob contributed his five minutes of instructions from the police department, Dr. Nisbit contributed his five minutes of instructions from the hospital, and then the press conference broke up. Bob left the press conference for his next stop.

The police station was a mad house. Stacey, bless her hyper and Post-It-happy soul, had appointed herself the coffee distribution specialist. Every police officer was sent out the door with stake-out level of food and drink supplies, as armored as possible, and with a full load of ammunition. There had been dark jokes for weeks about putting silver in the lead just in case, and Bob was pretty sure at least one deputy had taken the time to do just that.

At six o'clock, Sherriff Andrew appeared. He was due to retire in three months, but not due to any infirmities. Tough as a gnarled tree root, he gave a brief talk to each of the deputies. Many of them were steady men from around town who had lost their jobs when Missouri was cut off from the rest of the country. Each deputy received a firm pat on the shoulder and last-minute instructions disguising deliveries of confidence. Bob watched his fellow deputies head out for the most difficult night in their lives with strength and purpose.

"God, I hope I never have to do this again." Sheriff Andrew rubbed his forehead and leaned against Bob's desk. "Right son, you ready? You need anything?"

"No, I think I'm good. Stacey's provided me with the only thing I was short on. Smart, to save a bag for today."

"The ones who get stuck with the big chair have to think four or five steps ahead, not just two. Now, you have any idea where we find the boy and Ms. Mercer? We know they didn't get burned in her house after all, and we need to find that boy. He needs protection – both from Austin and from himself, tonight." Bob felt the firm hand and received the last-minute instructions. They arranged for alternate channels to use to call for help so that Austin's scanner wouldn't necessarily pick up a location. "It's not foolproof, mind you, so you'll still have to watch for them. But it's not as likely if it's not on the main channel."

"Got it, boss. I don't have any news, but I'll do a few look-in's and see if I can find anything. I'll be in touch." Bob gave his boss a firm nod of his own and left for werewolf patrol duty. The vehicle he got into to go on patrol didn't have the colors of a police vehicle. The only cars still moving were diesels powered by Missouri's home-brewed biodiesel industry. Bob's pickup truck had previously been used to haul pigs to the butcher to become bacon and smelled like pork and beer. He rolled down the windows and prepared to sweat through the July heat with no air-conditioning.

Bob had a list of addressed he'd gathered in the last week from reading club membership records at the YMCA. He drove to each of the members of the reading club that seemed to be Ms. Mercer's key social group, starting at the center of town and spiraling out into the suburbs. No one had seen Karen since the night her home had burned down, nor the boy she'd claimed as a grandnephew. Bob snorted, thinking of her public swoop to rescue the boy. The deputy had been sent out to detain out-of-state visitors, and Ms. Mercer had stepped right up to claim the boy was unknown, but local enough and HERS. Of course, anyone who'd sat through her description of Germany during WWII and Russia during Stalin's time in power should have expected it. No student who'd attended the local high school in the last forty years had been swayed by any of the fascist groups that sometimes rise in rural areas – Ms. Mercer was either in the back of their mind or there onsite protesting with a sign. In fact, it was because of Ms. Mercer that the local police and hospital had found an alternative to the "shoot on confirmation" that was happening in many other parts of the state. Bob didn't want to think about the number of innocent civilians who had probably been shot in the past 30 days because they couldn't prove well enough that they had been in Missouri on the night of past full moon.

The police band was active with reports of people taking advantage of the "call for a ride" number, asking to be in a restrained cage this night. Bob placed a little bet with himself that at least half of the people calling in to use the service were in no danger, they just wanted to be safe tonight from everyone else and had no other way of getting that safety.

The sun was already down when Bob approached his last hope — the cottage in the woods owned by the hippie member of the book club. The woman was reported to have never bought anything new, nor eat any vegetable that she hadn't grown in her own garden. Harmless lady, but crazy to leave Missouri in the middle of this madness. Deputy Bob was sure that checking this house would be a waste of time. It was empty long before Ms. Mercer's house had been burned down and had probably been ransacked itself weeks ago. It was also the furthest one away from Ms. Mercer's home, and there was no way a seventy-six-year-old woman walked all that way in the middle of the night.

The truck bumped lazily over the dirt lane, and the deputy saw smoke as if from a small campfire. He hit the brakes and reached for his radio. Fumbling to switch to the alternate channel, Bob reported, "Sheriff, I think I've found something at 312 N State Road 14." Per his discussion with Sheriff Andrew, he didn't stay on the radio. Backup was for normal times, not werewolf apocalypses. He checked his gun and got out of the truck.

"Ms. Mercer! Karen! It's Deputy Bob Ridley, ma'am! Please come out to talk if you can!" Bob slowly walked on the brick path from the dirt lane to the front door. He noticed that the door had been damaged severely but seemed to be closed now. Windows were boarded over or covered with sheet plastic. Away from his truck, his stomach growled approval at the smells carried to him with the smoke. "Please Ms. Mercer, I need to know that you're okay!"

"The last week has been as peaceful as possible in the middle of this riot." Bob spun to the left to face her. "I don't know as we want the trouble that is sure to come with you, though, Bob." Ms. Mercer was carrying a shotgun, but it was up over her shoulder. Her clothes were much too large for her tiny frame. Bob suspected that Ms. Mercer was wearing her friend's clothes instead of her own. The "grandnephew" that was no such thing stood next to her, in just boxer briefs. The boy looked different to Bob, but he couldn't place exactly why. There were sores on the side of his scalp that looked half-healed and a look of hostility in his eyes.

"Oh, thank God, Ms. Mercer. We just figured out that you hadn't died in your house fire day before yesterday. Do you have any injuries? Are you okay?"

Ms. Mercer brought the shotgun down, using it as a cane as she stomped towards Bob, spitting her words. "Well, now that you mention it Bob, I do have a few complaints. The fact that I'm uninjured and in clothes and getting asked about my health, while this young man who is nearly naked and scarred up remains not noticed by you is a problem. See, while you've been rounding up everyone who wound up in a difficult spot during a difficult time, some local boys have been beating the crap out of anyone you missed if they haven't killed them.

"So maybe I'd like to file a complaint, Bob, for the harassment against Tyler here, who was nearly killed waking me up and getting me out of my house that was set on fire by your precious Missouri Civilian Defense Association. You know, the group I tried to tell you was dangerous and you said, 'Sorry, Ms. Mercer, but the governor says we need the help.' Maybe I'd like to file a complaint for the arson to my home, and the loss of all my pictures of Frank." The tiny old woman stopped in front of the deputy, her fury almost a tangible thing. She also had made sure that she was standing directly between Bob and the teenage boy behind her. "If you take Tyler in, that stupid group of rednecks will come and kill me anyway. Didn't you learn anything in my classes? Austin is preaching us versus them to anyone who will listen. This boy is them and protecting him means I'm part of them. You're still part of us, part of the team, part of the machine.

"Get out of here, Bobby Ridley. Tyler and I need to pack up food and go."

"Ms. Mercer, please listen to me. The mayor is fighting Austin's boys. We were told to work with them tonight, but we're doing our best to work around them. I promise you, if they follow me here it's because they are monitoring all radios, not the just the police bands." Deputy Bob cried inside, that the woman who inspired the best in so many had become so isolated because the best of everyone else still wasn't strong enough to protect every person who needed it. "Please Ms. Mercer, we've established protective custody for anyone asking. We're making sure that they are protected from Austin's boys as much as making sure they don't become a danger to others. We really are trying Ms. Mercher, please." Bob looked over the head of the retired teacher in front of him to the boy behind her. It's the hair, Bob thought. He had one of those boy band hairdos and now all his hair is gone. "Tyler, I don't want you hurt any more than I want Ms. Mercer hurt. I promise. I'm trying to keep as many people safe through tonight as I can."

The boy looked back at Bob steadily. The hostility was less, but still not gone. His eyes moved to his protector. "I'll get the food ready and put out the fire. Be right back, Ms. Mercer." He ran back to the house. Deputy Bob noticed that his shoes were fashioned from duct tape.

It was just the two of them. A teacher and her student, once. Opponents in a war of someone else's making now, according to the way Ms. Mercer was eyeing him. He had to try one more time. "What happens if the boy does turn into a wolf again tonight, Ms. Mercer? He won't even know it when he kills you."

"Yes, we had a plan for that. He woke up after floating here on a boat, and we planned to put him back on a boat tonight. It seemed a reasonable way to isolate himself. He's very concerned. But since the governor passed that so very wise law to destroy all boats on the river, that option is now moot. Now we've an alternate plan. That's all you really need to know, Bobby."

Bob tried to engage her a few more time, but all his efforts were smothered by the blanket of her silence. The boy appeared around the corner of the house, eating something in one hand and carrying a canvas bag in the other. He nodded at Ms. Mercer. She turned to face him. "We're leaving now. Just take your truck and go." She walked to the boy and they walked back around the house towards the backyard.

Bob waited a few moments, letting them have their lead. He couldn't quite bring himself to leave as requested, despite his respect for Ms. Mercer. He was a local too, and thought he knew roughly where they intended to go. The full moon was only an hour away, by then. The deputy was too far out of town to be any good to anyone else tonight anyway. Being as discreet as possible, Bob followed the sound of their passage. As expected, they entered the woods bordering the nearby field that marked the boundary stream between the two farms.

Half an hour later and less than a half a mile away from the cottage, Bob heard another engine. His heart leapt into his throat when he heard the hound. Austin's boys were going to literally hunt Ms. Mercer and her charge. Ms. Mercer was right, Bob's call to the Sheriff had been overheard after all and disaster had followed him. It wouldn't be the boy who was the primary danger to the old woman any longer.

Deputy Bob turned toward the mob of men following the hound. He had decided to tail her to protect Ms. Mercer. He would shield her as best as he could from the greatest threat to her life. Even if it meant getting in the path of a mob ready to kill.

He scanned the dark field, looking for any advantage for one man facing a group. But this was a flat soybean field. There was nothing higher than his knees, and plenty of things to stumble upon. The only advantage he had was his authority, and he was desperately afraid it wouldn't help him at all with this crowd. He pulled his gun and his flashlight. He scanned the woods one more time before turning around. He thought he could see Ms. Mercer being lifted into a giant oak at the edge of the field. There was an angular shape to the leaf canopy of that tree. The truth hit Bob. They've put a camping hammock in that tree for Ms. Mercer. Wolves can't climb trees.

Bleakly, he turned away. There was louder crashing behind him as Tyler took off at a run. The deputy turned on his flashlight and addressed the approaching crowd. "Good evening gentlemen. Can I help you?"

Muzzle fire bloomed in the darkness, and Deputy Bob was thrown back. His flashlight highlighted the face of Greg Striefer, Austin's younger brother. His snarl was meaner than any wolf's. The local farmer stopped long enough to grab the deputy by the shirt front and hiss, "If you're trying to hide foreigners from us, then you're trying to help a wolf. Damn you to hell for sacrificing my family to some demon." He shoved Bob hard against the dirt.

Then he was gone, running to catch up to the hunting party. Deputy Bob Ridley was left with nothing but a mangled, bleeding leg and the sounds of the hound baying in the distance. Bitterly, Bob prayed that Tyler did indeed turn into a wolf who could take on the lunatics   hunting   him.

HECTOR THE WEREWOLF
By Patrick Handlon

Hector sat on the bed in his basement bedroom among the piles of dirty clothes, comic books, and video games. One could say that he was a typical teenager except that, around a year ago, he had turned into a werewolf. He sat reflecting on that day, as he had done many times before, and wondered, no, hoped, he would turn into a werewolf again. Even though he wasn't quite sure what happened when he was a werewolf, he was sure it was the coolest thing that ever happened to him. While he had heard that some of the people who had turned into werewolves last June had killed people, he was sure that he wasn't one of them.

Hector however, wasn't one much for thinking. He wasn't the sharpest tool in the shed, the brightest bulb in the lamp, the wisest owl in the woods…..well you get it….While Hector received average grades in school they seem to be awarded mostly for good attendance rather than anything else. For instance, despite the fact that he received a C+ in geography, and that he had seen numerous globes in his classrooms and pictures of the Earth taken from space, he still believed that the world was flat. He would lie very still at night so as to not tilt his bed one way or the other and fall out. He also held the theory that the Earth was hollow and for some reason could not see the contradictions in the two theories. Hector, to put it as nicely as possible, is a moron.

Proof of this came six months ago, when the government started seeking out people who had turned into werewolves, Hector walked down to the City County building and turned himself in. Mr. Carson, the janitor at the City County building, wasn't sure what to do but they eventually figured it out. He was convinced that the government was creating a werewolf super team and he wanted to be in on the ground floor. He was whisked away in a helicopter to a top-secret research facility in Missouri. The helicopter ride would have been the greatest moment in his life if he hadn't already turned into a werewolf. Missouri was determined to be the safest place to house the facility as no one in Missouri had turned into a werewolf and those who had turned into werewolves stayed away from the place like Hector stayed away from deodorant. He had read an article on the internet that it caused cancer. Well, his friend Chad had read the article or a meme or whatever but he still believed it.

Hector was disappointed to find that the top-secret facility was an abandoned high school and not an impregnable fortress built into a mountain top. No one at the facility had the heart to tell him that there were no mountains in Missouri. Again, the C+ in Geography seemed suspect. The research facility proved to be more boring than Hector had thought it would be. Much like his time at his high school he spent a lot of time sleeping as there was nothing better to do. He was prodded and poked by doctors and assorted scientists but there was no training for a werewolf super team. In fact, after a series of tests that included a physical and an intelligence test, he was mainly left to his own devices. All around him other former werewolves were hustled to various tests but not him. So, he wandered the facility. He went to the gym to shoot hoops to see if his werewolf powers made him better at basketball like Teen Wolf but he still missed every shot and was slower than ever.

He walked the halls undisturbed. He was beginning to think maybe he was invisible but that was proven wrong when he forgot to wear pants one day. As a fly on the wall Hector was privy to more information than the other test subjects were. He overheard conversations that he shouldn't have, wandered into areas that were restricted, and watched two hours of a close circuit autopsy that he thought was a television show. Unfortunately for the other test subjects Hector could not connect these bits of information to see the bigger picture but, fortunately for them, the cafeteria did not stock the mini chocolate donuts that Hector liked to eat for breakfast.

Early one morning Hector walked out the front door of the highly guarded government facility, through guards, reporters, and looky-loos, to the neighborhood convenience store. He loaded a handbasket up with his favorite mini chocolate donuts, nacho chips, and strawberry soda. It was only when he reached the counter that he realized that he had no money. Everything that he brought with him to the facility had been confiscated when he arrived. It had seemed odd to him that the government would take his money but since he had been working a part-time job at Dairy Queen, he was used to the government taking his money and handed it over. Hector told the man at the counter about his involvement with the super-secret werewolf project at the old high school and that the government had his money. The man at the counter didn't seem especially eager to let Hector put the food on the government's tab. What he was interested in was knowing what was going on at the super-secret research facility in the old high school. So, in exchange for Hector's recollections of everything that he had seen at the facility, he was given two packs of mini chocolate doughnuts and a strawberry soda. Hector thought this was an especially good deal and left happily but, when he returned to the facility, the guards wouldn't let him back in. They said that they didn't recognize him. Hector borrowed a reporter's cell phone and called his mom to come and pick him up. She was a bit upset that she had to drive to Missouri to get him but was secretly overjoyed that he hadn't been picked to be part of a werewolf super team. Hector's mom wasn't really bright either.

At home Hector was looking for anime on a local television station and saw the nice man at the convenience store talking to reporters. The man was telling them everything that Hector saw at the facility without mentioning Hector. He kept talking about an "inside source" and Hector sat on the couch watching and wondering who the "inside source" could be. It was probably the lady in the cafeteria with the big mole, she seemed sketchy. At the end of the interview the man asked for the money he had been promised for the interview. Hector wished he had been so lucky to be on television and get paid for it. Even though he didn't get paid or get picked for the werewolf super team life went on for Hector. He still went to school every day, received nearly straight C's on his report card, and always got picked last for basketball in gym class.

And so, Hector sat on the bed in his basement bedroom among the piles of dirty clothes, comic books, and video games. He removed his Battlestar Galactica shirt and stared at his chest. He felt that any day now he could turn into a werewolf again. The hair that appeared the day after the werewolf incident was growing and starting to appear in places other than his chest. He also noticed that his voice was beginning to change, getting deeper like a werewolf's. If only he could remember the day he had turned into a werewolf but he had fallen asleep after a 24-hour Twilight Zone marathon and couldn't remember exactly what happened after that. He just knew that he had woken up hairier than normal and groggy. Still, he was sure it was the best thing that ever happened to him and couldn't wait for it to happen   again.

WEREWOLF MOSH PIT
By Jonathan Byrd

Sam strung the final chord to his band's closing song and the crowd of rowdy teenagers applauded. Several of them were so engaged in the mosh pit they didn't even notice the song had ended and continued to push against one another to the fading amplifier feedback. A couple of bored adults stood toward the back of the small grange hall, arms crossed, eyes glued to their phones, or rechecking the only clock in the room which read 8:15 pm.

At that moment a brick crashed through the windshield of the vintage Volkswagen van Sam's band the Surfing Goats used to travel around the tri-state. The van had been a gift from Sam's oldest brother when they learned their parents were getting divorced. Sam had spent the previous summer with his grandfather, a local automotive salesman, fixing up the rusted old van into semi-working condition. The sound of glass breaking was lost in the noise and it would be another 20 minutes before Sam would realize what had happened.

Outside the venue Thomas smiled at the broken windshield. Fragments of glass glittered on the gravel parking lot, reflected by the lone light hanging over the entrance of the grange hall. He watched the door to see if anyone had heard the noise. Thomas was strong, tall, and quick. Prior to destroying the Surfing Goats van, he had only used these advantages for sports, primarily football where he excelled so significantly he had received a full-ride scholarship. After scanning the area and seeing no one he darted behind the building to find the back entrance. He came to a sudden stop when he encountered a group of girls in catholic school uniforms passing a lit cigarette in the dark.

"Captain," one of the girls said with a sarcastic salute.

Damn, they'll know it was me now, Thomas thought.

"Good evening ladies," Thomas said with a nod. "Is the back entrance over here?"

"There is no back entrance," a familiar voice said from the dark. Kelly stepped forward and Thomas felt an invisible punch to his gut. It has been only a few days since the two had ended their years-long, on again-off again romance. The sight of her caramel brown skin and pink hair in the darkness sent a chill down Thomas' spine.

"Funny," Thomas said. "This is the firefighter's grange hall, isn't that against their own fire ordinance?" The girls laughed. They were about to perform next, their all-girl synth punk band, WYTCH35 was very popular and they were usually the local closer for any rock show.

"You'll have to go around front," Kelly said. She flipped her hair while extending a hand to receive the cigarette. She took a single puff then flicked it onto the sidewalk. "We're about to go on so you might wanna get in there, we have some new songs you should stick around for."

"Great," Thomas said, "I'm heading in now, let's see what you have to say about me in these new songs."

Kelly laughed. "Well aren't we vain this evening? We go on at 8:30 so get your butt in there if you wanna spot near the front."

Inside the venue Sam and his band bowed to a cheering crowd. He walked to the side of the stage where each band kept their equipment, there was no backstage, only a supply room behind the stage filled with tables and chairs primarily used for community fundraising spaghetti dinners. He packed up his guitar as Kelly and her band walked into the supply room. He smiled as she approached him in her band uniform. She smiled back.

"Great set," Kelly said. "You gonna stick around for ours?"

"Wouldn't miss it!" Sam said. "I'll be out there, right after our post-show ritual."

"Weed?" Kelly asked with a smirk.

Sam shrugged. "It helps me unwind."

"Yeah, sure, but your brain isn't fully developed yet, you should wait until your mid-twenties according to the most recent science."

"I know. You've given me this speech before but the world is literally ending as we speak. I may not even be around to see my mid-twenties at the rate this rock is heating up."

It also helps me avoid thinking about my parents' divorce and the effects that is having on Dot, Sam thought but did not articulate. Sam's little sister Dot was currently across town with a babysitter. Their parents were both out on a date, but not with each other. They seemed to have a silent but ongoing competition to see who could move on faster. Sam was tired of them both and was excited to finally leave at the end of the school year. His older brother promised him a room in his Baltimore apartment for the summer while he figured things out. Sam's only fear was leaving Dot to be pulled apart by their two narcissistic parental units.

"Well, good luck dude, I mean Kelly," Sam said, "Not that you need it, you guys are great- I mean girls, you girls are great."

Kelly covered her mouth to hide a laugh. Sam blushed.

"You should consider taking a gender studies class in college, Sam," she said.

"Yeah, okay. I will," Sam said before awkwardly adding, "I'm gonna walk away now."

Sam's bandmates were waiting outside, already passing a joint.

"Did you ask her out yet?" one of them called.

"Shut up," Sam said, grabbing the joint for himself. He sighed, realizing they had smoked almost the entire amount without him. "I'm finishing the rest, see you guys inside." The sound of Kelly's band warming up filtered out the grange hall entrance. Several teens were finishing up their cigarettes and walking back inside. Sam took a walk along a line of trees behind the building, breathing in the cool air and watching the sky fade from an orange red sorbet sunset into the black of night. He laid on the ground for a moment and stared up into the sky. The light of the full moon bled its way through the clouds, illuminating the ground.

I wonder if I'll be able to see the stars in Baltimore, Sam

thought. I should look up into the sky more often, it just goes on forever, kind of like our brains too. Like I'm the exact middle of everything. I can project both outward and inward forever if-

"Hey!" someone called from the parking lot. "Sam! Someone broke into your van!"

Dot hid behind a large blue recliner. The one her dad used to sit in while everyone else watched TV. He would sit and read and mumble about things. Now the chair was usually empty. Her dad had moved into a small apartment across town and only came by a few times a week. Mostly to yell at her mom it seemed. She heard heavy footsteps enter the living room followed by a low, heavy sigh. The shape walked slowly, examining the room. Dot held her breath, trying her best not to be discovered. She lowered herself into a crouching position so it would be easy to stand up and run. Adjusting herself behind the chair she bumped into its back. Squeeeeak, squeeeeak, squeak, her dad's blue chair whispered. It was enough for the shape to lunge at the chair. Dot screamed.

"Found you!" Lisa, her babysitter yelled. "Now seriously, it's time for bed Dot. Go brush your teeth and pick out a book. I'll be right there to tuck you in."

"Okay," Dot said sadly. She slowly walked towards the stairs.

She turned abruptly to challenge the babysitter, "But it's only 8:20, I don't go to bed until 8:30, and that's ... TEN minutes!"

"Yes Dot, very good, but it ought to take you 10 minutes to get your little butt up the stairs and brush your teeth now won't it?" Lisa said with more patience than Dot was accustomed to receiving.

"Okay," Dot said walking up the stairs. She brushed her teeth, chose The Octonauts & the Great Ghost Reef from her bookshelf, and sat on her bed. The clock now read 8:27. Dot impatiently flipped through the pages of the book she'd read hundreds of times. She decided to play a prank on Lisa and stood behind her bedroom door.

The clock read 8:30 when the sound of lumbering footsteps entered the upstairs hallway.

This is perfect, Dot silently laughed.

She stood behind the door listening to Lisa walk closer to her room. A low growling now accompanied the loud, slow steps. Dot did not recognize the sound. They did not own a dog and the neighbor's dog, which she seldom heard while inside, was a tiny chihuahua that only yipped and never growled with such a deep voice. She remained frozen and silent, determined to get the upper hand after Lisa found her hiding spot so easily before.

The footsteps stopped outside Dot's bedroom door. The growl faded and was replaced by a loud sniffing.

That's definitely a dog, Dot thought. How did a dog get in here? I better see what it is-

A large hairy figure jumped into the room, shaking the floor so badly Dot fell to the ground. It ran to her bed and tore at the sheets with two enormous claws and the largest jaws Dot had ever seen up close. Dot covered her mouth to muffle a scream.

"Why would anyone do this?" Sam said. His van was ruined. Shattered glass lay all around over the dashboard and front seats of the van.

"I don't know," Kelly said. She had heard about the incident and came out to check on Sam. Inside the grange hall her band was warming up. Random drum fills and bass riffs floated out into the night. The low hum of the crowd inside talking was as steady as the chirps from the crickets outside.

"I guess I'll call one of those glass companies," Sam said, taking his phone out of his pocket. "You should head back inside; I know a lot of people are pumped to hear the new shit."

Kelly nodded. "If you're still here later let me know, we're recording the set so I'd love for you to hear it if you have to miss it now."

Sam smiled. "That would be most excellent, thanks Kelly."

Kelly turned and walked back towards the grange hall. Her mind was elsewhere, thinking of Sam, thinking of Thomas, and realizing it

was probably Thomas who did this out of spite. So it took her several moments to realize the sound resonating from the hall was no longer talking and absent-minded chords. It was screaming.

Inside Thomas was making his way to the front of the room when people all around him started falling to the ground.

"See, that's why I never eat anything from the food truck," Thomas said, walking past another person who had just slumped over. "And what is everyone screaming about? I mean seriously-"

The body on the floor was growing. Thomas saw buttons fly across the room as they grew large enough to rip their clothing.

"Hey man, you okay?" he said, reaching down. He patted the person on their back then recoiled in disgust. Their entire back was covered in thick, gray hair. Thomas screamed. He turned to run out the door and saw the bizarre bottleneck of people with the same idea, and other hairy creatures attacking anyone around them.

Thomas grabbed a metal folding chair and threw it into a window. Glass shattered into the room and the creatures turned their attention towards him. The crowd took advantage of this opportunity to exit the building. One of the creatures followed. Thomas jumped out of the broken window and rolled his shoulder against the wet grass. He stood up and took off running.

"Sam!" Kelly called.

Sam looked up from his phone, his face illuminated by the search results for local glass repair companies. Kelly was only a few steps from the entrance when a flood of people began running out of the grange hall. They were all covered in blood. One of Sam's bandmates stopped outside the door and vomited onto the sidewalk. An adult emerged and screamed.

No, that was a roar, Kelly thought. She began running back towards the van.

The adult was completely covered in hair. It swiped from left to right with two enormous hands. The creature knocked a few fleeing teenagers to the ground. It lunged at one Sam recognized as his bass guitar player. His friend screamed. The creature lifted its jaws.

Chunks of meat fell from its open mouth. It howled.

"Quick, get to the van!" Sam yelled.

All around them people were running and screaming.

Howls echoed in the night as other creatures responded to the first.

Thomas ran through the field, edging his way closer to the back of the parking lot. He saw Kelly running towards Sam's van.

"Start the van, we have to go!" Kelly said.

Sam took off his jacket to wipe glass off the passenger seat.

"Get in the back," Sam said, "there's glass everywhere." Kelly jumped into the back of the van. She grabbed the door to close it but felt the weight of someone holding onto it. Thomas threw himself into the van next to her as Sam turned the engine over.

"What the hell are you doing here?" Kelly said.

"Surviving," Thomas said.

"Hold on!" Sam yelled. The van peeled out of the parking lot, dodging people running towards their own cars. In the rearview mirror he saw the creatures regrouping. He counted at least ten standing in a circle, edging their way closer to a large group of humans.

The ones who didn't transform, Thomas thought, His mind replayed the horrific scene from only a few minutes ago.

Kelly held onto her legs and buried her face between her knees. The sound of humans screaming in terror echoed through the night and slowly disappeared as Sam drove the van into town.

The thing that was Lisa had torn up the mattress searching for Dot. It then moved on to the closet and easily hacked away at the particle board doors. While the thing that was Lisa had its back turned Dot lowered herself and quickly crawled out of the room. She stood up in the hallway and moved as quietly as she could to the stairs.

Claw marks cut deep lines into the walls all along the staircase. A few paintings had fallen onto the ground, frames broken and canvases slashed. Grandma's paintings, Dot thought sadly. She jumped over the mess and down the stairs. She walked to the door and unblocked the handle. Gripping the door with her small, five-year-old hand, she pulled. It was stuck. The deadlock, several inches above her head, was locked as well. The stool! she thought.

Dot made her way to the kitchen to locate her stool. It was not in the usual location by the sink.

Mommy must have hidden it after she caught me stealing fruit snacks, she thought. Where does mommy hide my stool? Dot checked under the sink, using her index finger to press down on the child-safety locks. She looked behind a bottle of rum, wasp spray, and a container of bleach, but did not find the stool.

A loud THUMP rang out from the entryway. The thing that was Lisa was walking down the stairs. It paused to sniff after every other step.

It's smelling me, Dot thought. How can I hide my smell?

Dot reached back under the sink and grabbed the bottle of bleach and the wasp spray. Mommy's not going to like this, she thought while opening the bleach and pouring it around the kitchen. She then opened the door to the basement and silently closed it just before the thing that was Lisa peeked its head into the kitchen.

The creature sniffed the air then sniffed the ground. It growled at the foreign smell.

Dot held her ear to the basement door.

The creature howled.

Dot screamed.

———

"What the fuck is happening?" Thomas asked.

His question lingered unanswered. Sam drove towards his home, located just outside of the small town of Smithsburg. His only thought was on finding Dot. Kelly sat in the middle seat of the van. Her hands were still clutched around her knees. Her black, curly hair obscured her face. She continued counting down from 100 in her mind.

72...71...70

"Where are we going? My house is the other way!" Thomas shouted.

Sam turned the van with such force Thomas and Kelly fell over in their seats.

"We're going to find my little sister," Sam said.

69...68...67

"No way, let me out now, I need to get home," Thomas said. He wondered where his parents were, they had planned to get dinner somewhere but he couldn't remember what they said. He was glued to his phone, per usual, and nodding along but not really listening.

"You can jump out, but I'm not stopping," Sam said.

66...65...64

Thomas sighed, "How far away are we?"

"Just over this hill," Sam said. "Lisa is babysitting her, so I'm hoping she's okay, but, god, what if..."

"What if Lisa turned into one of those... creatures," Kelly said.

"Or even a neighbor," Thomas said, "Look, I get it, but I have family too Sam."

"Well, it was my fucking van you jumped in, right?" Sam yelled.

Sam turned the car too quickly again, this time veering left into an open field.

"Are you crazy?!" Thomas yelled.

63...62...61

Sam drove the van down a steep hill. smashing a fence at the bottom into pieces. Fragments of wood shattered against the van and flew through the giant hole where the windshield used to be.

"Sorry," Sam shouted, "but I know these woods, and the fastest way to my house is down this hill." They continued the bumpy ride across diverse terrain. Thomas grumbled to himself. Kelly continued counting down in her mind until the van stopped.

"Are we here?" Kelly asked. She looked out at the dark yard. It was completely still and silent aside from the chirping of crickets. A bat dove overhead near an outside house light, snatching a large moth and flying away.

"Yeah, this is my house," Sam said.

"I know. I remember," Kelly said.

Sam and Thomas turned to her in shock.

"I guess you don't remember," she continued. "We used to be good friends, you know. In like fourth grade or something, I used to come over here all the time." She examined the house, her brain flooding with memories. "I remember that stone fence you have, remember when we hid behind it with water guns and shot at cars?"

Sam laughed. "Oh yeah, you really nailed some businessman who stopped his convertible and ran after us."

Kelly laughed.

"Can we speed this up please?" Thomas asked with visible annoyance. "I have people to search for too you know."

Kelly sighed.

Sam unbuckled his seat belt.

"Okay, I'm going to look for Dot," Kelly said.

Before either Sam or Thomas could argue she jumped out of the van and ran to the front door of Sam's house.

The thing that was Lisa smashed into the basement door sending Dot down several steps. She rolled off the side of the staircase and into the finished section of the basement her family used as the kid's rec area. She rolled onto the couch and landed on the floor in front of their small tv with a built-in VHS player.

Oh my god, she thought, before smashing the play button on the tv with her tiny fist.

The screen came to life, flooding the room with a white light and a loud ROAR. The VHS inside the tv was set to the scene in Jurassic Park when the t-rex escapes its paddock in a thunderstorm. Every time a large thunderstorm rolled in Sam would grab Dot and head to the basement, turning on the movie at this exact scene as the real-life thunder boomed all around them.

"Surround sound," Sam would joke.

Dot wondered where her brother was.

The thing that was Lisa broke through the basement door.

The T-Rex on screen roars at Dr. Grant.

Dot crawled away from the tv, into the unfinished half of the basement.

The creature jumped down the stairs towards the television.

"Ian! Freeze!" Dr. Grant shouts.

Dot heard static and sparks as she crawled behind the washing machine.

The thing that was Lisa howled in frustration.

Upstairs the front door opened.

––––––––

Kelly walked into the house and closed the door on the sound of Thomas and Sam arguing about what to do next. She examined the surroundings and laughed inside her head.

Everything looks the same, just smaller, she thought. It had been several years since Kelly had been inside the house, Dot was a newborn, and Sam was a lanky, pimple-faced pre-teen. As was I, she thought.

A roar echoed from the basement. Kelly walked towards the sound. The basement door was no longer attached to its frame. Pieces of broken wood and metal lay across the kitchen floor. She took another step towards the basement. The pounding of footsteps filled the room. Before Kelly had time to react the werewolf ascended the stairs and stood before her. Its large yellow eyes stared at Kelly who found herself unable to breathe.

How is this possible? she thought.

"Lisa!" Kelly shouted.

The werewolf tilted its head at the sound.

"It's me Lisa, it's Kelly!"

Lisa sniffed the air.

"We have home economics together Lisa, you know me!"

Lisa took a step closer. Kelly took a step back.

Lisa barred her teeth and lunged at Kelly.

"We can't just sit here," Sam said, "it's my house and my sister we're looking for."

"You let girls walk over you, huh?" Thomas smiled.

Sam scoffed and stood up, "Go to hell Thomas, I'm going in-"

Thomas reached both hands over Sam's shoulders and slammed him back into the driver's seat. Sam realized if it came to blows, he wouldn't stand a chance against the captain of the football team. Hell, I've never even been in a real fight, he thought. The closest he ever came was a few years back while carrying an electric guitar into school, some senior called "Hey! I heard you suck!" and Sam's quick-witted retort was "I heard your Mom sucks." Within moments Sam was apologizing while the senior considered whether it was worth detention or not to kick his ass.

"Here's what I'm thinking Kelly's game plan is, as her former boyfriend I have some experience in these things. We're the getaway crew. She's gonna run out here with ... sorry, what's your sister's name again?"

"Dot."

"She's gonna run out here with Dot, and we'll have the van all ready to go, and hopefully we won't be chased by one of those wolf monsters."

Thomas raised both hands to his temples in mock explosions, sarcastically indicating this was an amazing plan.

"Okay," Sam said. "Maybe you should grab some weapons just in case we have to fight off one of those things."

Thomas examined the van from side to side. "What weapons Sam?" he said, throwing up his hands. He grabbed an empty water bottle, "Maybe I can smash this against a monster's head?"

"There should be a baseball bat in the shed. It's never locked, just head over there," Sam said, pointing to the small shed next to his house.

"That's the first smart idea you've had all evening." Thomas stepped out of the van and made his way across the lawn to Sam's shed.

Sam collapsed his head against the steering wheel. I am way too high for this shit, he thought.

———

Dot crouched behind the washing machine and listened to the noises upstairs. Someone had entered the house and was talking to Lisa. I know that voice, Dot thought, Sam listens to her music all the time. The floor shook as bodies fell somewhere in the kitchen. Dot stood up behind the washing machine, ready to run.

I need to get out of here and find Sam, Dot thought.

A high-pitched scream echoed throughout the house.

The thing that was Lisa howled above her.

No, I need to help that girl, Dot thought.

She walked towards the stairs, noticing the bottle of wasp spray lying in some debris from what used to be their basement door. She picked up the wasp spray and slowly began ascending the stairs, hopping from right to left to middle, aware of which areas to avoid creating noise. Pieces of broken door made this more difficult than usual.

Dot reached the kitchen and saw a girl lying on the floor.

She turned her head around looking for Lisa.

She stood still and silent, listening for any movement. In the background the shed door slammed shut.

Good, it's outside, Dot thought, walking closer to the girl on the floor.

"Are you okay?" Dot whispered to the girl.

The girl moaned and sat up.

"Dot?" she said, "I'm Kelly, I'm here to rescue you."

"I know you," Dot said, "You sing that song that my brother listens to all the time. I know all the words."

Kelly laughed then winced.

"It's always great to meet a fan. Now we need to go, your brother is outside."

"Okay," Dot said, "Can you walk? Are you hurt? Are you okay?"

"One question at a time kid," Kelly said, reaching for the counter and standing up. Dot tried to help but realized Kelly was covered in a mixture of bleach and red paint. Oh god, that's not paint, she thought.

"You are hurt, let me get the bandages," Dot said. She walked to the medicine cabinet and located the two items her mother always used to heal Dot's wounds. A dark brown bottle, a yellow tube, one cotton ball, and a box of band aids.

"Wow, you're very resourceful," Kelly said, taking the items from Dot.

"What does resourceful mean?" Dot asked. Kelly's pink hair was the brightest thing in the kitchen. Dot watched as she cleaned out a bloody scrape on her waist.

"Oh god," Kelly moaned, while pouring liquid from the brown bottle against her skin. "I'll explain in the van, we need to go now." Kelly placed several band aids over the wound, then covered it with her shirt. Dot reached for Kelly's hand as they walked into the foyer to head outside.

The doorway was blocked by the creature. Blood dripped from the creature's claws over the floor. White teeth flashed against the moonlight pouring into the house. It took one step.

Dot raised the wasp spray and pressed down on the nozzle. White liquid shot out into the creature's face.

The creature howled and fell to its knees, kicking and slashing at everything around it. A small table in the foyer fell over, spilling family trinkets across the floor.

Kelly placed her hand over Dot and began walking backward towards the kitchen when a figure emerged from the open front door. A baseball bat came crashing down on the creature's skull. Pieces of bone, brains, and blood spewed all over the foyer. Dot turned and buried her face into Kelly's stomach.

The baseball bat made loud, wet sounds. Hot liquid landed on the back of Dot's legs.

When the pounding finally ceased, Dot's crying covered the

silence in the room.

"My god Thomas," Kelly whispered. "You killed Lisa."

Dot let go of Kelly and turned around to see the creature lying still on the floor. She watched as the body turned back into the shape of the babysitter she was so fond of. The huge hairy arms rescinded into the thin, hairless arms that had chased her around the house only an hour ago. The body of Lisa lay on the floor of the foyer, no longer a monster but the Lisa everyone around her knew. Everything about her was back to normal, except for her head.

Dot slowly came to realize the object on Lisa's shoulders was not a broken watermelon.

―――――

Sam heard Dot screaming. He jumped out of the van and made it to the front door as Kelly was carrying his sister outside.

"Is everyone okay?" he asked.

Kelly nodded, her cheeks stained with tears. She placed Dot on the ground who embraced Sam. She continued crying.

"I want mommy," she said.

Sam exchanged glances with Kelly.

"We'll go find them, right now," he said. Sam picked up his sister and carried her to the van. He placed her in the seat and buckled her in. Thomas appeared next to the group, his shirt was stained dark red.

"Any sign of Lisa?" Sam asked.

Thomas walked out of the house. His shirt was stained dark red.

"She's gone," Thomas said. He sniffed and wiped his eyes against his sleeve. "Look, I had no choice, it wasn't Lisa at the time-"

"It's okay Tom," Kelly said, grabbing his hand.

Silent tears rolled down Thomas' cheeks.

"Okay, let's go find your family now Thomas. You helped me out here, I want to help you out too."

Thomas nodded a thank you and the three friends walked back towards the van.

The van sputtered in the background against the otherwise quiet evening. In the distance sirens and otherworldly howls were offered up to the moon. In Sam's mind all the noise seemed as far away as the moon itself that hung like a giant glowing rock in the sky.

"So where to?" Sam asked before his entire property was lit up in blinding white light.

A voice shouted through a megaphone, "No one is going anywhere!"

————

"Who are you?!" Sam shouted. Dot unbuckled herself and ran back to Sam's side.

"Have any of you been bitten?" the voice shouted.

Sam looked at Kelly and Thomas. It was hard to tell whose blood was on who at this point.

Until I check if they've been bit, they've both been bit and not been bit, Sam thought, unconsciously replaying a discussion from his physics class earlier that week.

"No! No one has been bit!" Sam shouted.

"Okay!" the voice shouted. Sam heard muffled discussion sneaking its way through the hot mic of the megaphone.

"We're taking you to safety, get in the van children!" the voice shouted.

The white light dissipated as Sam, Dot, Kelly, and Thomas were surrounded by black uniformed soldiers. Their faces were covered in tinted riot gear helmets. White mist rolled out of the van door as it slowly opened.

"We have to disinfect you before you can get in the van. Oh shit," Sergeant Bowers said removing the megaphone from her mouth. "Sorry, how rude, I'm Sergeant Bowers, kids I'm here to escort you to Raven Rock." The thirty-something year old woman extended her hand to Thomas then took an immediate step back when she saw he was covered in blood.

"Wait, who's blood is this?" she asked.

"A little is mine, most belongs to our friend Lisa, but she wasn't Lisa anymore-" Thomas pleaded.

"It's okay son, where is the body?" Sergeant Bowers asked.

Thomas turned away and walked towards the van.

"It's in the house," Sam said.

Placing the megaphone back to her mouth Sergeant Bowers shouted "In the house, people, go collect samples."

Dot covered her ears.

"Ugh, I did it again, I'm so sorry little girl," Sergeant Bowers said. "What's your name honey?"

"Dot," said Dot.

"Well Dot, I'm going to take you, and some other new friends you'll meet on the van, up into the mountains where we'll all be safe, okay?"

"Okay," Dot said. Sam put an arm around his little sister and walked into the mist.

Kelly followed until Sergeant Bowers placed a hand on her shoulder.

"And you? Whose blood is this?" she asked.

Kelly caught a lump in her throat. She coughed.

"Lisa, it's mostly Lisa, maybe I got scratched by something while the house was being destroyed but I swear I'm fine," Kelly rambled.

The Sergeant gave her an up and down look before nodding her head towards the van.

"Go on, get cleaned up, you'll be examined by our medical staff upon arrival."

Kelly stepped into the disinfectant chamber. The door closed as white mist was sprayed in all angles at her body. As the liquid seeped into the cut on her side she cried out in pain. She felt her side twitching in frustration. She lifted her shirt and saw her wound bubbling, and oozing white and dark red liquid from her side. She gasped in horror, and pulled her shirt down lower, holding it there as the mist subsided and the second van door opened.

"Welcome to the Raven Rock express, sweety," the bus driver said, gleaming down at Kelly as she ascended the stairs to safety.

———

The van was completely full of people. Some Kelly recognized from her small town, others she had never seen. Some were quiet, staring out the tinted windows. Others were huddled together and crying. Kelly sat in an empty seat a few rows behind Sam, Dot, and Thomas. She found a Smithsburg Leopards sweatshirt beneath the seat. She rolled it up and placed her head against the van window. She pretended not to hear Thomas and Sam talking as she drifted off.

"Raven Rock," Sam said. "I wasn't even sure it was real. But apparently the government built this bunker during the cold war, and employed an equal number of dudes and chicks in case the world ended in a Fallout style nuclear holocaust. They could live underground and repopulate the earth. There's like a whole city there, a food court, even a freaking fire department."

"Here!? In the redneck, backwoods hills of this state?" Thomas said skeptically.

"Camp David is here too you dummy," Dot said. She yawned and placed her head on Sam's shoulder.

Thomas laughed. He stomach churned at the thought of something happening to Dot, this little girl he just met. He felt sorry for her and Sam, not knowing where their parents were. He wondered where his own parents were now too. He took a deep breath, preparing himself to take a huge bite of humble pie.

"Look, Sam, I'm sorry for throwing a brick through your windshield man," Thomas said. "I was just...angry I guess, that's too simple though. Losing Kelly was the final straw. Especially to a goddamn white dude!"

Sam exhales, "I get it, but I also had no idea dude-"

"It's not that man, I'm just so tired of losing out to mediocre white dudes!"

Sam scoffed, "Wow! I'm mediocre huh?"

Thomas ran his fingers through his hair, searching for the right words.

"Look man, how much time did you spend getting ready this morning, huh?"

"I put deodorant on, that's about it."

"Exactly! That's all society expects from you Sam! I have to try twice as hard for people to even consider taking a second glance my way, and I'm the captain of the goddamn football team! You roll out of bed and society opens its arms to embrace another white boy who doesn't even have to try to make it in life. Do you understand Sam?"

A third voice cleared their throat. Sergeant Bowers stood over them.

"I'm sorry to interrupt such a spirited debate regarding race relations, especially since I'm a woman of color myself, but I need to get you all up to speed. When we arrive at Raven Rock, we need to take Dot and Kelly with the other females, but I assure you that you'll all be reunited very soon."

"No," Dot said. "I'm not leaving Sam."

She held on tight to her brother's hand and stared defiantly into the eyes of Sergeant Bowers.

"Yeah," Sam said, "we're staying together."

Sergeant Bowers closed her eyes and sighed, "If anyone asks, I'll say you escaped." Then, raising the megaphone to her mouth she shouted to all the passengers, "Our destination is five minutes out, please grab any belongings you may have, and prepare to exit the van. Males and females will be separated and reunited shortly after physical examination."

The loud voice startled Kelly awake. She saw Sam, his long blonde hair raggedy and matted from the night. Thomas sat beside him, cracking jokes and making Dot smile. Kelly reached into her pocket to retrieve her phone. She located an mp3 file named The Two Wolves and sent it to Sam and Thomas' phones. Kelly was excited to perform her new song in front of her two flames but she knew that would never happen now. She wondered what became of her bandmates as Sergeant Bowers stopped beside her seat.

The van continues driving up into the mountains. Kelly viewed the beautiful Appalachian countryside, taking in its beauty in a way she never had before. The moon still hung large in the night sky, bathing the trees and mountainside in its white glow. Before she knew it, the van had arrived at a large gate. The bus driver spoke to the guard at the entrance for a few moments before they proceeded to drive underground. After several miles the van parked in a large car garage.

"It's time to go ma'am."

Her friends stood to stay goodbye.

"I'll see you there," Kelly said. She gave a small wave. She met Sam's eyes and returned his smile. She nodded at Thomas and he nodded back. "Oh, and check your phones" she called.

"This way ladies," Sergeant Bowers shouted through her megaphone. Dot lowered her head from view to avoid being absorbed into the group. Kelly walked off the bus with Sergeant Bowers and the rest of the females, a group of about 20 women that included children to seniors.

"Since you've all gone through the decompression chamber, we can lead you right to your rooms. They're just up this elevator. You gals are about to get the only outdoor view in the whole facility! The elevator has a new moonroof. Over the years we've received too many complaints about being underground so this was recently added."

Annoyed by the lack of appreciation, Sergeant Bowers raised her megaphone and added "You're welcome!" at full blast.

Kelly laughed as a few of the girls shrieked.

"Oh god, sorry," Sergeant Bowers said. "I'm trying to make things light but I realize many of you have been through horrific experiences this evening. My apologies."

"Rawr!" screamed a little girl.

Sergeant Bowers pretended to be scared.

"There's one now!" an older woman called. "Quick get it!"

The group of women began to relax around each other, making gallows humor of the terrible night they'd somehow survived.

"Okay, calm down everyone. Let's step into the elevator. You're going to get a close-up view at that beautiful moon."

The women filed into the large elevator and stood shoulder to shoulder.

Sergeant Bowers let the youngest, a girl around Dot's age, press the button that sent the elevator upward. As they ascended the women were flooded by the white light of the moon.

Kelly felt her skin begin to crawl. Her body felt cold and tingly. She rubbed her arms for warmth and noticed an abundant amount of hair.

Good lord, she thought, Do I need to start shaving my freaking arms now too?

"Here it comes ladies!" Sergeant Bowers said.

"It's like Willy Wonka," a little girl called.

The women in the elevator laughed as Kelly transformed from a petite teenager in a catholic school uniform to a gigantic wolf creature. The force of the transformation shoved all the women into a corner of the elevator. Sergeant Bowers reached for her hand gun. The werewolf began slashing and tearing into the women. Its huge teeth tore chunks of flesh out of the elderly woman who stood closest to Kelly. The woman screamed and fell to the ground, blood spilling out of her open wound and covering the floor of the elevator. Sergeant Bowers fired a shot that ricocheted off the elevator wall and through her own forehead. She fell dead on the floor. Women screamed all around. Within a few seconds, everyone inside of the elevator was dead.

The werewolf stood, covered in blood, still devouring bits of flesh from the pile of meat on the floor. So hungry, it thought. It was such a small amount of food; the creature would have preferred nothing. Now its hunger was only stronger.

ONE MORE TIME AROUND

By Aaron Farrow

June 22nd, 2024

It was a warm June morning, and Eric woke up to the opening theme to *Dexter's Laboratory*, just the same as he had all four years in high school. He liked to sleep with the TV on; it gave him something to do when his recurring bouts of insomnia woke him in the middle of the night. There was some magic about that wordless opening jingle that pulled him out of whatever sleep he had managed to find, gently letting him know it was time to get up and get ready for school.

Except now there was no more school. Graduation had changed it all. Now every morning just felt strange. Unlike some of his other friends Eric had no idea what he wanted to do with the rest of his life. For the first time the future seemed to be a mystery. The familiar cycle of school and summer vacation was broken, and Eric found himself staring down the barrel of a lifetime of uncertainty. Nothing had changed physically. A hot June morning was the same as it ever was, but inside everything felt wrong. Broken. Strange.

Eric was a stereotypical teenager. He ate garbage but still maintained a 125-pound, scrawny frame. His dark brown hair was thick and shaggy, often unkempt. His typical attire consisted of heavy metal t-shirts and jeans with a pair of Airwalks strapped to his feet. Despite the affinity for skater clothes, Eric wasn't athletic or capable with a skateboard. It was more about identifying with the outsider culture.

Eric got out of bed and looked around the room. The walls were covered in posters for video games going back ten years. His TV stand was littered with game consoles and DVD's strewn about in a labyrinthine mess that only its owner could understand. This was the room of a teenage boy who dedicated himself to geeky pursuits, priding himself on his knowledge of fictional worlds and the various heroes and villains within.

He left his room and wandered down the hall into the kitchen of his parent's split-level home. After making a bowl of cereal, he sat down at the bar and turned on the NES that was hooked up to a small TV hanging from a cabinet. It was time for yet another speed run of Contra. The classic game was notorious for its steep difficulty, but Eric had mastered every input. Playing through it was no longer challenging but relaxing. The repetitive button presses had become routine, making it a kind of meditation for him. The fog of life was less threatening here. The world was simple and it had a simple objective. He loved the order and clarity. Within them, there was focus.

Today was going to be a good day. Eric was going to meet up with his old high school gang for what was likely to be the last time. Robert was leaving for art school, so they had decided to have one last get together. Joe would be there. Like the rest of them he was quiet and shy. It seemed he was destined to be a local tax accountant, but unlike Robert he was at peace with that fate. Rounding off the group was Dave. He loved horror movies and had a notorious short temper but was a good and reliable friend.

After completing his first run of Contra and looping back to the first level, Eric heard Joe pulling into the driveway. He always did get going earlier than the rest of them, the only one that didn't adopt the teenage gamers' penchant for sleeping until noon. Reliable and mechanical, almost like a nice stopwatch. He had always been the one most worried about never getting a girlfriend. He cared deeply about what others thought of him. Joe often sought refuge at Eric's house while his parents continued to fight through their bitter divorce.

Joe was the cleanest cut of the crew. He kept his light brown hair well maintained by frequenting the salon in the mall. This meticulous habit made him the butt of many of the group's jokes. While he didn't have an athletic build, Joe wasn't as scrawny as Eric. His attire was better too, but he still had an affinity for band shirts. While Eric was fond of Metallica and Iron Maiden shirts, it wasn't uncommon to see Joe sporting The Clash, The Who, or The Cure instead. Just like the rest of them he maintained an interest in older movies and bands.

"I knew you'd be the first one here, you old man." Eric said playfully. Of their little group, Eric and Joe had been friends the longest, all the way back to third grade.

"I knew you'd have something smart to say, slacker. We can't all sit around eating cereal and playing Contra. At least I know you'll never change. Rob's probably going to go off and get a bunch of fancy college friends now."

Eric and Joe went down the steps to the driveway and climbed into Joe's car. Unlike Eric and the rest of the gang, Joe kept his car neat and clean. This usually made Joe's car hands down the best option for group outings. The plan for the evening was simple enough. Get the crew together, go out and get some food, and then sit in the parking lot of their high school and close this chapter of their lives. It was nothing fancy, and none of them wanted to make a huge deal of it, even though they all somehow knew that this was the end. There was just a feeling in the air, like everything was about to change.

The next order of business was the drive out to the poorer side of town to get Dave. They pulled into the gravel driveway of an older row home. Unlike the rest of them, Dave's family was on the lower side of the middle class. They weren't poor but also couldn't afford the latest and nicest things. Sometimes this made Dave jealous of the others, especially Robert. What little money Dave could get his hands on was spent on his only vice: horror movies. He lived to find films more obscure and violent than the last. He was a walking horror film Wikipedia page; his knowledge of the genre being almost second to none.

Dave kept his blonde hair short and spiky. His build was slim like the others, but he was closer to Joe in size. He too liked to advertise his fandom to the world through his clothing. Unlike the two awaiting him in the car, Dave preferred to be decked out in horror clothing. More often than not it was a Halloween shirt, mainly because Michael Myers was his favorite horror villain of all-time. He sauntered out of the house and jumped in the waiting car. "What up pimps! Are we ready to get this show on the road? Might as well get our final party over with before it all falls apart on us. Don't get all weepy on me though. Might as well tear it up one last time. If you can call what we do tearing it up anyways." Dave was always a mix of excitement and pessimism.

"Ha-ha, don't be so dramatic man. We'll have plenty of time to hang out. School won't be in the way anymore. You ready to go get Rob?" Eric was used to diffusing the more negative aspects of Dave's character. Without him taking the edge off, Dave wore on the other two. Eric was often the mediator of the group. In many ways he was the glue holding their motley little crew together.

With that, the three of them were off to get the man of the hour. Robert lived in a nice neighborhood, where the large houses were separated by huge, cultivated backyards. His family had moved around a lot, and they often resented living in suburban Pennsylvania. They were a left-leaning family, and the rural life was beginning to take its toll on them. Robert enjoyed a nice upbringing. He shared the group's common interests in horror, sci-fi, anime, and video games but was still the outsider among them. He had a taste for the finer things, and he wasn't going to settle for anything less than what he wanted from life. He was an easy addition to the group though, as they all bonded over their mutual interests. More than that, they had bonded over their mutual enemies, the jocks and popular kids. The ones who hated them for no reason other than they were different. Nothing will bond teenage boys better than a shared hatred. High school was a battleground, and together they had survived.

Robert was the shortest and thinnest of the four. His shoulder length brown hair was often unkempt. He would usually wear shirts sporting bands of various genres, horror films, and anime. Robert was also the least concerned with what others thought of them. All senior year he wore a pair of increasingly worn bicycle gloves everywhere he went. People thought he did this simply to shock and offend others. While this was part of the reason, it wasn't the whole story. Robert was confident in who he was. It was important that others see him in whatever way he saw himself. There was something freeing in the way he was willing to let go of the confines of social pressures.

The three of them pulled up the large drive and parked in front of Robert's four car garage. They were pumping Metallica's *"Master of Puppets"* as loud as the little factory speakers of Joe's 1995 Mercury Cougar could manage. This was their last hurrah. None of them quite knew what was happening, but they all felt it. After tonight, nothing would ever be the same.

Robert came out of his home pretty quickly, and the four of them loaded into the Cougar and set out for Denny's. It wasn't fancy, but for four years it had been their haunt. It was a pretty junky one too. The staff had notorious problems with heroin addiction, but it was familiar to them. Routine. A fitting venue for their final meal as a high school posse. Like many other teenagers with odd social habits, ritual was important. Denny's was a soothing constant in a world that was facing them with a lot of change.

"I'm gonna order the Bea Arthur slam." Robert quipped. The group had a disturbing love for The Golden Girls, and anything they could work into a pun based around the show was gold.

"Come on man, don't do that. It's embarrassing. You're going to make them spit in our food." Joe lamented. He wasn't one for drawing attention to himself. His ideal evening was one where they all flew under the radar.

"I dare you. Dooooo it. Do it." Dave encouraged. He loved watching Joe squirm. It's funny how often friendship and rivalry so closely border each other. As if one bad day was all that separated friends from being enemies.

The meal was one for the record books. Unlike most evenings, the food was on time and fresh. The four of them laughed and joked, and then everyone ordered dessert. All that was left was to decide what to do next. That idea came from Dave.

"Hey, why don't we go kick around the old school a bit? What better way to celebrate the end than to finish where it all began?" he said in his usual snarky manner. Robert wasn't too sure about this idea.

"I thought that was the plan. That's what he talked about earlier." Dave replied.

"I'm about to spend four more years in school. Why would I want to go back to my old one? Plus, we all hated that place."

"It wasn't so bad. Some of our best times were in that school." Joe replied. Walking through the past was something that was right up his alley.

"Joe's right." Dave agreed. "So let's stop being limps and get back to being pimps."

They argued about it briefly but soon the foursome all agreed to stick to the original plan and revisit the old high school. They piled back into the Cougar and drove a short distance from Denny's to the high school. The four of them decided to sit down on a small field by the auditorium and reminisce. Time passed, and the sun began to set. Slowly, the full moon rose into the sky. "I just wanted to thank you guys for coming out." Robert said. "I don't know what it's going to be like with me off at school. Dave isn't right about much."

"Screw off man!" Dave playfully jeered.

"…but he is right that it will be harder for us to get together from here on out. It means a lot to me that we all got to get together before I finally get the hell out of here. I know most of you guys like it here, but I hate it. The people here are backwards. I think a change of pace is exactly what I'm going to need."

"I hope you find what you're looking for dude. It won't be the same without you around. I'm glad we decided to do this and hang out before you run off." Joe was the first to offer his well wishes while the other two nodded in agreement.

"Well on that note guys, it was fun but it's about time we split." Eric said. "As much as I love sitting around this place, I think we can do something more interesting. Maybe we can go back to Robert's and watch some DBZ or some horror movies? Nice and predictable, just the way we like it. We wouldn't want to rock the boat too much, now would we?"

Out of nowhere, Skylar and Joel staggered drunkenly over the top of the hill. These two had been a thorn in the crew's side their whole lives. The two of them came from broken homes and had begun drinking at the age of 13. It wasn't uncommon for them to chase Eric and Joe through the park when they were both 12, attempting to knock them down and piss on them. Neither of them had managed to finish high school.

"Well, well, look who we have here. What a nice coincidence. I needed a few people to beat on." Skylar said menacingly. He was the living embodiment of a high school bully.

"Come on you assholes, back off. We were just leaving anyway." Eric protested. Dave took that as his cue to run. He went booking over the hill and out of sight, leaving the three of them there to face the bullies alone.

"Great, just great. Thanks Dave." Joe lamented. None of them were well equipped to fight. Their fighting skill was mostly centered on fleeing, ducking out of trouble or techniques learned from video games.

Night had descended upon them. There was something different about the darkness. The sense of unease was palpable. Nothing looked different but this eerie feeling set everyone on edge. The small hairs on their arms were standing up, and it was hard to shake the feeling of someone walking across their graves. This night was different. It had something horrible in store.

Skylar cracked his knuckles and approached Robert, Eric, and Joe, a nasty smirk spreading across his face. Joel was a few paces behind him, gleeful at the opportunity to watch the violence. This wasn't uncommon; Joel had always been Skylar's lackey. It was a cruel twist of fate to come back here to the school just to revisit the old balance of power. Dave's suggestion had worked out terribly, and he was the first to bail out.

Just then Skylar's face burst into a mix of surprise and horror. His eyes bulged out as a spray of blood burst from his mouth. Horrible claws tore through his mid-section, dousing Eric and Joe with his viscera. No one quite knew how to react. The moment was frozen in time. A hulking wolf-like form stood behind Skylar, burrowing a huge hairy arm through his back and out his stomach.

Eric was the first to snap out of it. Covered in the gory remains of Skylar's insides he looked like something straight out of *Carrie*.

"What the hell is that thing?! Come on let's move, we have to get the hell out of here!"

With that, the three of them ran as fast as they could towards the school doors, not knowing what to do when they got there. They just knew they had to get away from the wolf creature. Joel stayed behind with the remains of his friend that was being torn apart. Limbs, bones, and sinew were being tossed about in random directions as the creature ravaged Skylar's corpse.

They were almost at the doors now. Looking back, they saw another one of the creatures bound out of the darkness and sink its jaws into Joel's throat. His death happened in an instant as blood erupted in an arterial spurt that flowed through the second wolf's teeth like crimson rapids over rocks.

Luckily the doors were open, and the three friends burst through them and into the halls of their high school. Joe slammed the doors shut behind him and engaged the locks, backing up as quickly as he could from them. The trio stood in the empty, locker-lined hallway, staring at each other in disbelief.

"Ok...ok...what... I don't even..." Joe gasped, trying to catch his breath and make sense of what they had just seen.

"I think it was a... werewolf." Robert said what they all were thinking, even though it made no sense. Werewolves weren't real. Sure, they were real enough in an *American Werewolf in London* or *Dog Soldiers*, but this was real life. This couldn't happen.

"Whatever they were, what do we do now? We can't go back out this way. I better call the cops. In the meantime, let's back away from these doors." Eric tried to use his phone to call the police, but it wasn't working. Either the circuits were busy or whatever strangeness had taken hold of the night was interfering with the signal. It didn't matter which was true; it was clear that help was not on the way.

"I think we should just go through the school and go out the back. Maybe they'll stay up the way we came. Plus, we know our way around here. There should be plenty of places to lay low. That could be used to our advantage." Robert suggested.

"We won't be able to get to my car that way." Joe replied. "Maybe we can just keep an eye on them and go back outside when they leave."

"I think Robert's idea is the best. We don't need the Cougar. We'll just bolt out the back and head for someone's house. Maybe their phone will work and we can get help that way. Or, if that fails, we just do what Robert said. Find a classroom or something and lay low, maybe one of the shop classes that don't have any windows. We could board up in there if it comes down to it." Eric offered. It wasn't much of a plan, but it was better than standing around and waiting for those horrible creatures to return.

"Well Joe, you always did like a trip down memory lane. Let's get the hell out of here." With that statement Eric, Robert, and Joe began to cautiously walk through the darkened halls of their old school. Everything felt familiar yet also out of place. These strange feelings grew with the deepening shadows as they each contemplated the horrific ordeal they had just witnessed. It was at that moment that the distant wail of police sirens became apparent. They hurried into a nearby classroom and looked out the window. Nothing could prepare them for what they saw. A police cruiser careened across the street and crashed into a nearby house. There were about thirty people fleeing through the yards pursued by eight wolves. The sound of gunfire and screams rang out into the night air under the pale glow of the full moon. Carnage and gore were strewn about like a war-torn battlefield, and blood began to fill the streets by the gallon.

"Holy shit." Robert gasped. "I don't think leaving here is such a good idea anymore. We can't go out in that. Just look at all of them. There's so many…"

"Yeah…alright. We're going to need a plan. The school seems safe enough. Maybe we should just wait it out. What are the rules for werewolves? Are there rules? The moon is full, so that lines up. Maybe if we just hang out here until morning we can leave and try and figure this all out." Eric was trying to calm down, but his heart was pounding in his chest. He had a problem with anxiety, and this was not helping at all.

"Rules? I don't know if this is like some kind of movie. How does that even make sense? We don't know if they'll go away in the morning. We're so screwed. We shouldn't have even come here. What the hell were we thinking? Where's Dave? Holy shit guys he might still be out there. What are we gonna do?" Joe was in full freak out mode and beginning to get loud.

"Calm down dude, calm down! They might hear us. We need to get away from these windows. Maybe we could head upstairs towards one of the corner classrooms. Something we can block up nice and tight. I think that's a better idea than the shop class. This way we're on the second floor. Maybe they won't come up that far if they don't think anyone's up there. That's gotta be better than sitting out here in the open, especially since we don't have any weapons." "Doubt we'll find much in the school. Especially since the rednecks aren't here." Eric had managed to calm himself down enough to think about their situation. They needed a plan. A goal.

Joe pulled Eric aside as Robert continued to stare out the window at the bedlam in the streets. He was transfixed, lost deep in thought.

"Yeah… I guess you're right. I'm not surprised Dave ran out on us. He always was an asshole." Joe had calmed down, and some of his resentment at Dave's constant picking was beginning to bubble to the surface.

"Come on man. Don't say that. Dave's just Dave. That's the way he's always been. He's always been our friend." Eric countered.

"Maybe, but he's still an asshole. I keep thinking about how he said this was the death of our group. He's been moaning about that for the past four months. Maybe he is right. I hope he's alright out there but… maybe this is the end. Assuming we even get out of here alive. This school isn't holding us together anymore. Whatever happens to the other guys… whatever happens tonight, just promise me we'll always be cool." The gravity of the situation made Joe's words sink into Eric more than usual. Despite the situation, this was important.

"Yeah man… I promise. We've always been friends, always will be. Don't talk like that. We'll all be friends after this. You'll see. Now let's get moving. I don't think it's such a good idea to hang around here."

The three of them moved through the school towards the stairwell in blackness. The main power had gone off at some point and the school and surrounding neighborhood was blanketed by darkness. The only sources of light came from the nearby fires and sirens that illuminated the first-floor classrooms in flickering light. It felt as if they had been taken back to the stone-age. Much like their ancestors, the teenage boys cowered in darkness from the threat of unspeakable predators.

A set of fire doors further down the hall began to shudder with loud thuds. Something was smashing into them with terrible force. They groaned under the stress and bulged inwards, threatening to break loose at any moment.

Suddenly, the doors burst forth and a slathering monster erupted into the hallway. Its fur was dark grey and matted with blood. Its eyes had the cold deadness of a shark that was hungry for more fresh meat. It sniffed the air searching for someone to kill. It was only a moment before it turned its gaze down the hall at the cowering friends.

"Run!!!" Eric screamed at the top of his lungs, and the three of them sped through the stairwell doors and clambered up towards the second floor. They could hear the wolf skitter across the waxy floors as it burst into a full gallop. It skidded across the floor and collided with a row of empty lockers, bending the doors and leaving them in a crumpled heap. It wasn't much, but they hoped this momentary delay would buy them the time they needed to get away.

They ran through the second-floor hallway and bolted for a corner room, just as they had originally planned. Spilling into the room, Joe once again slammed the door shut behind him. All three of them dropped to the floor and crawled back away from the door, hiding beneath the rows of desks. They didn't know if it had heard them come this way. They hoped to God that it hadn't. Their only option now was to wait in terrified silence. None of them dared to move in an effort to barricade the door. No one made a sound.

The wolf's labored breathing could be heard outside the door. Its dark shape moved past the door window. Everyone held their breaths. The beast pressed its nose up against the glass and let out a blast of hot air from its nostrils, fogging the window. The game was up and they all knew it. This was the end.

To their surprise the sound of gunfire echoed down the halls outside the classroom. The beast screamed in unnatural agony as a splash of blood spattered across the door's window. They heard a whimper, then the slump of a large body against the door.

"I think someone shot it." Joe said in a whisper.

"Sounds like it. Can that kill them? Don't you need silver bullets or something? One of us should go look. Eric, maybe you should do it." Robert replied softly.

Just then the door creaked open and the bloody frame of a police officer entered the room. "Hello?" he said, "Is anyone in here?"

"Officer, what the hell is going on?" Eric was the first to rise to his feet, somehow willing the terrified things to lift him off the ground.

"No one knows, but we have to get out of here. These things are everywhere. Bullets work just fine on them, but I don't have nearly enough. We need to get to my cruiser a few blocks over and get out of town. Now if we're lucky we can make it to the army depot. Are you boys ok to move?" The officer's explanation didn't clear much up, but at least it gave them a plan.

"Yeah officer, we can move." Robert spoke.

"I just want to go home guys. I just want to home…" Joe looked defeated.

"Don't worry… we're getting out of here. All of us. Let's move." Eric was desperately trying to rally his terrified friends. It would all be worth it if they could make it to the officer's car. It was their only hope.

The four of them moved past the slumped form of the werewolf as they moved back into the hallway of the school. Following the current plan, they headed to the opposite end of the school and down the other stairwell towards the west end exit doors. All that was left was to step out into the horrors of the night and make for the officer's cruiser and the promise of safety. With a little luck, it could be as easy as it sounded.

They spilled out into a scene of pure horror. Screams rang out in the distance amidst unnatural howls. Bodies lined the street in varying states of dismemberment. Some moved slightly, spending their last moments moaning in agony. Otherwise, the coast was clear, for now.

"All right. My cruiser is right over here. We need to run as fast as we can. Don't stop for anything. Even if one of us goes down."

It was then that one of the monsters came tearing out of a nice suburban hedgerow, full of terror and fury. The officer tried to raise his weapon, but there was no way he could match the speed of the beast. It tore into him with rage and hunger. Bones splintered like toothpicks and the officer gurgled, a foamy mist of blood coming out of his gasping mouth. The surviving crew had trouble summoning the courage to flee. Their sure-fire escape plan had crumbled before their eyes in a flash of crimson agony. They didn't know what to do. They all stood there, deer caught in the headlights. A row of little red riding hoods helpless before the big bad wolf. Lambs lined up for the slaughter.

Joe was the closest to the wolf and was quickly caught by its thrashing limbs. It hadn't even paused to consume the slain officer but was functioning out of pure bloodlust. The teen tried to fight the beast, desperate to keep its gaping maw from hitting home and ending his life. He flailed about at the creature as claws tore through tendons and exposed bone to the cool night air.

"No! No! Help, please, please… get it off, get it off!"

Robert and Eric remained frozen in place, watching their long-time friend as he was ripped apart by something straight out of a horror film. Their time with him flashed within their minds. An entire life of friendship played out in an instant. They felt regret. A lifetime of loyalty and there was nothing they could do but stand by and watch him be killed. He had always said his high school years were the best of his life, and now he would never live to find the validity in that statement.

Eric snapped out of the daze. It was too late for Joe, who was being reduced to an unrecognizable pile of bloody mush, but it was not too late for him. He dove for the slain officer's sidearm, knowing it was his only chance. At the same time Robert took off in the opposite direction without saying a word. The second friend in one night to abandon him. He didn't care anymore. Joe had been his best friend and he had failed him. He was torn and conflicted about what had just happened. Had they all been friends for real? It had felt real enough but now he wondered if they had only been friends through their mutual enemies. All of those thoughts quickly cleared from his mind. Now there was only one thing left to do. Vengeance was Eric's only thought. He didn't know how he was going to survive the night, but he was going to kill this thing.

The house to his right was on fire, flames casting a hellish glow on Eric's blood-stained form. His face was blank and emotionless.

He had dialed into a level of primitive survival instinct. Nothing was going to stop him. He raised the gun and fired three shots into the monster. It howled in agony as the impacts pushed the creature back from the eviscerated corpse below it.

The beast charged Eric in response, slamming into him full force and launching them into the burning building. It had once been a nice home, but here in this world those things had lost all meaning. Now it was a burning hell. A world in which only two existed.

Part of the roof collapsed, burying both of them in burning rubble. Eric coughed in agony. Some of his ribs were surely broken, but somehow, he found the will to rise. He picked up a flaming beam and began flailing at the creature before it could rise again. It howled in agony, slashing its furious claws blindly in Eric's direction. None of the hits were fatal, but the blows tore Eric's shirt and drew blood as the claws skimmed flesh. The two stood there in their primitive contest, each slashing at the other, determined not to rest until the other was dead.

The floor lurched as part of the first floor began to fall into the basement. The werewolf started to slide first, and reached up to grab Eric's leg. He was powerless to break the grip, and they both began to slide downwards into the depths of hell itself. Eric looked to his right and saw the gun sliding down as well. He made a quick, desperate grab for the weapon and was overjoyed when he wrapped his hand around it. He knew this was his only chance. He aimed it at the creature's head and fired into its skull as the two entwined foes crumbled into the basement with the rest of the home. Now there was only silence and the slow crackle of flame.

The morning sun began to rise some hours later. The sound of birds began to chirp across the silence. The town looked like a warzone. Whole rows of homes were burned to the ground and bodies dotted the street. People began to come out of their hiding places, looking around in dazed wonderment at the chaos all around them. Although they had survived the night, none of them could yet believe or make any sense of what had happened.

Eric's eyes slowly peeled open and the blinding sunlight felt like a thousand daggers piercing him at once. He was surrounded by the cinders of the home where he had fought the beast. Somehow, he was alive. Shooting pain began to course through his whole body. He knew he had broken ribs and likely a leg. He looked around, taking in the scenery. He wanted to make sure the wolves were not still lurking around in the daylight, hungry to finish the job.

To his shock he saw a body to his immediate right. It was where the monster had fallen after he shot it in the head. Only the form lying there wasn't a monster at all. Sitting there in a bloody mess, filled with sharp splinters and a skull that was broken open like a melon was a human body. What did this mean? Eric knew he had fought a wolf. He had seen it. The marks left by claws and teeth attested to that fact. The events of the night before had strung him out completely. His eyes fought to recognize the body, but his mind wouldn't accept the truth. It was hard to make sense of anything, let alone form coherent thoughts. He felt tired, battered, and alone.

A group of paramedics spotted him amongst the rubble and pulled him out onto a stretcher. They explained to him that the hospitals were very full, but that he was going to be ok. They told him that this had apparently happened nationwide, and no one knew why. He heard them talk about how all the wolves had disappeared, and that the dead ones had changed back into their human form. No one remembered if they had turned into one of those things, or if they did, they weren't telling anyone. Eric didn't care anymore at that point. He had survived. Exhausted, he allowed himself to drift off to sleep.

BOY SCOUT NIGHTMARE
By Casey Little

Under the covers of my dinosaur bed sheets, I rocked my feet back and forth. "Tomorrow is my birthday", I whispered to myself. I pulled the sheets up over my head and giggled. I was sooo excited!

"Dad said there was going to be a surprise for me. Mom is baking a hot fudge cake because it's my favorite; how can anyone hate chocolate?" I said to myself.

Peeking out over the top of the covers I looked over at my T-rex nightlight, then the little league baseball trophy my team won a couple weeks ago. Some of my teammates would be coming to the party tomorrow. I wondered what I would get. I love opening presents so Christmas and birthdays were my favorite times of the year.

"You better be in that bed Zack." Creaking open on old hinges, the door revealed Mom as she entered my room.

"I am, Mom," I drawled, "but I just can't wait till tomorrow."

Mom sat on the edge of my bed and ruffled my hair with her hand.

"Well then Dino-boy, you better get to sleep because it's almost 9 o'clock and you have a big day tomorrow." She smiled.

Leaning over she gave me a hug and then kissed me on the head. "Goodnight, I'll see you in the morning." she said as she got up from the bed.

As she was leaving my room Dad grabbed her hand and spun her around by lifting her arm over her head. It looked like they were dancing and I grinned. Mom was short and really pretty, but Dad was tall and kind of scary looking. Dad was really nice, though. I guess the scars on his face that he got from the car accident just made him look kind of scary to other people. I thought he looked really cool.

"Travis!!" Mom laughed and slapped Dad on the shoulder. She reached up and pinched his nose. He had to lean down a little so she could reach his nose and raised both of his hands, "You got me Officer Lori. I give. Punish me as you see fit. Boil me, fry me, throw me into a stew, but please, ohhh *PLEASE*...don't burn me like you did the Turkey last Thanksgiving."

Mom arched an eyebrow. "Oh, I'll do something to you alright."

Dad gave me the 'HELP ME' look and I laughed shaking my head.

" Dad! You just had to bring up the Turkey."

Dad let his hands drop and dangle with a defeated look on his face. "Two against one, that's not fair." he murmured.

Mom let go of his nose and shoved him into my room. "Come on, he's got a big day tomorrow. Go say goodnight." she said.

Dad grinned, stood up straight and then jumped on my bed being careful not to land on me.

"DAD!" I screamed laughing.

"I'm going to eat you little boy", Dad said lowering his voice as he crawled up from the base of the bed, "and I will huff and puff and blow your toes off."

I pulled my legs to my chest, getting my feet as far away from him as I could. He stopped and then swung his legs over the side of the bed and he reached out ruffling my hair just like mom had done. "Goodnight Dino-Dude, I'll see ya in the morning."

I laughed, "Okay Dad, Goodnight."

He got up from the bed and joined Mom out in the hall. Before they closed the door I called out, "Mom, Dad?"

The door opened again and Dad poked his head back in the room.

"Yes?"

"I love you."

He smiled "Love you too."

Mom opened the door and peeked in as well. "But I love you more." She shrugged and slyly glanced at Dad. "Just so you know." Mom smiled at him and then winked at me.

"How do you know? I think I love him more. Humh." Dad said snapping his fingers three times in the air in the shape of a z.

Mom rolled her eyes, "For the record, when I was giving birth you totally wussed out. You had to leave because you almost fainted." she said and then disappeared down the hall.

"Did not!" Dad said slightly offended. "I held your hand 'til the end, thank you very much. For the record, I didn't almost faint, I just got a little lightheaded and had to sit down. By no means did I '*almost faint*' thank you very much."

Dad started to follow her down the hall then popped back into my doorframe.

"G'night birthday boy. See ya in the morning."

I slid deeper under my covers.

"Goodnight Dad."

Dad pulled the cord on my lamp and then closed my door. The room got darker, except for the little glow coming from my night light. I wasn't scared of the dark, but I couldn't sleep without it yet. Like Dad couldn't sleep without the ceiling fan on. He told me that it was kind of the same thing.

I looked at my stegosaurus clock which read 7:51pm. I rolled over onto my side and closed my eyes. Before I knew it, I was asleep.

...

I sat straight up in bed. "What was that?"

I didn't really remember what it was that woke me but whatever it was it was really loud and high pitched. All I knew was that it scared me out of a dead sleep. I felt my heart jump up into my throat and my stomach knot. I didn't know what this feeling was, but I didn't like it, not at all.

I looked around the room and listened. Nothing had changed in my room except for the clock that now read 9:30pm, and I didn't hear anything else.

The hair on the back of my neck stood on end and I had a feeling that was telling me to hide. I was scared. No joke. I was shaking and I wasn't cold. Dad had told me about what to do if I ever felt something so strongly and couldn't ignore.

"Listen to it." Dad had told me. "That feeling is called instinct and it is something that can save your life. It saved mine during the car accident."
So I did.

I flipped the covers off my legs and swung my feet over the side of the bed and onto the floor. I stood and stacked my pillows where I had been laying on the bed to make it look like I was still there, then covered it up with my covers.

I grabbed my baseball bat and hid in my closet. I reached up to the knob and locked it from the inside. Mom told me to never lock it since I had accidentally locked myself in there when I was younger. But I was sure she would be okay with it now since I knew how to get back out.

I found the stack of blankets, that we used during the winter, and slid under them. Just in case the doors were somehow opened, I wanted to be hidden.

"Think smart, stay calm," was a saying in Boy Scouts. My dad had been a boy scout when he was small, and he thought I'd enjoy it, plus it would be good stuff to know.

Well, I was sure using it now.

I had left some space so I could still see but keep my face hidden. I could also see out of the grooves on the bottom of the closet door. I had just gotten comfortable when the door to my room opened.

I didn't get a clear view of the thing, but it was some kind of large animal with dark brown fur. It smelled like a dog. Its size was weird, so I continued to watch. I focused on my breathing to keep calm because we were taught that animals were sensitive to fear, especially if they were predators.

I heard a low growl come from the creature, and then there was a massive crash. The legs of my bed buckled and cracked, then fell to the floor. All I saw was white stuffing go flying, lots of it.

There was a snarl and then some kind of roar as shredded dinosaur covers fell to the floor. Then it all stopped. There was a thump and then a shadow fell over the closet doors. I controlled my breathing, but just barely, and noticed the dog smell grow thick.

It was mixed with a sour smell that I had only smelled once before when we were looking at a deer Mom had hit on the way home. It was the smell of blood?
Was that blood?

"What about Mom and Dad!" My mind screamed.

My breathing increased and my heart jumped back up into my throat.

I panicked.

There was a brief flash of yellow and looking through the crack were two large eyes staring at me.

Crap, I panicked! I messed up!

The closet doors rattled and then cracked as they were being pushed in.
I squeezed the grip of my bat.

"Swing wide, swing strong." That's what my baseball coach had told us before our big game and that was the only thing that could help me now.

THE LAST TURN
By Cody Grady

I decided to end the incessant whining long before I had the courage. The problem wasn't in the deciding, of course; making a choice is easy. In an emergency situation every animal chooses with blinding speed. Human beings differ because they wallow in the decision, pondering consequences and eventualities. Yet place any person in peril and the choices come easily. Adrenaline courses through a racing heart as arteries vibrate like a single, plucked guitar string; muscles tense and breathing deepens, all in preparation to act. In that slow, self indulgent moment of expectation, the mind chooses without thought of provocation or repercussion. The strain becomes too much; the bough breaks and the cradle falls. Then you find yourself falling over the edge. It isn't the decision making that is hard. Overcoming Fear is the real bitch.

I grasped frantically behind the rack that ran from floor to ceiling. The packed equipment made it impossible to see through, so I tore at the back blindly. After a moment, my hand grasped a bundle of coiled, organized cords. Without hesitation I gripped tight and pulled. Plastic groaned and then snapped, giving way freely. Pulling my hand away, I saw the mess of cable wrapped around a clenched grip. Though it must have been several moments of silence, the serene noiselessness of the room didn't dawn on me until now. The unceasing and emotionless drone had come to an end. Glancing back, I saw the red light no longer stared out at me from its black box; the evil, bloody pupil had died out because it could no longer feed itself. I felt myself trembling, partially from excitement yet also from electrocution, I supposed, noting that sensation for the first time. I didn't care. For the first time in hours, I was in control.

Willpower is the key. To find the inner drive to move forward, to achieve and accomplish. The decision, the Fear, the self-loathing: all of these can fuel you, push you to the very edge of the precipice... all the way to the edge of existence.

Yet standing at that height, toes curling off the edge of comfort and safety into the open air of uncertainty, doubt begins to creep back in. It settles like a lead weight in your bowels, causing you to question. Then the mass climbs its way up through the stomach all the way to your throat, dragging along an acidic tasting bile. Suddenly inner fire is extinguished by nerves; Fear saps the resolve. And so we stand there with the known behind us and oblivion before us, waiting for the Will to plunge forward or the Fear to step us back.

I turned around, checking the readout to confirm what I already knew. All the needles had fallen against the side walls of the meters. I was not crazy. No one else was hearing the voice now either. Looking across the dimly lit room through the glass, I could see the side of the control room was still bathed in red and white reflections of the LED sign mounted above the window on the other side. Though I couldn't see it, the other room glowing a demonic rouge was all I needed to know. We were still "On the Air". The station was now broadcasting Silence.

In time, though, even Fear loses its effectiveness. Like a war-ravaged amputee you begin to accept dark feelings that once caused such strong, vitriolic emotions. The body copes and the mind forgets. Scar's form, healing the exterior, as inside you distance yourself from pain. Fear is no different, and as you stand above the unknown, you accept, find comfort in, then ultimately ignore the terror. Swaying with the breeze on the edge of it all you become raw... numb to Fear. So why still do you not act? Fear has been conquered; the sadomasochistic pleasure once derived from it is gone. So why now do you not step forward? Or choose to turn away from the fall?

Inside, the truth becomes evident. You question your inaction, ponder its significance. The mind tears itself apart searching for the Will to execute, or, finding its absence, contemplating the significance of its nonexistence. A voice inside begs a question that must be answered. Why won't you pull the trigger?

Dead Air was the worst. A professional faux pas that is not easily forgiven. Listeners accept long commercials, bear less than enjoyable content, and suffer through the obnoxiousness of a single, repetitive tone. But not Dead Air, not Silence. It's unnatural for a radio to not emit auditory output. The eerie sensation caused by silence soon turns to dread as the listener is forced to contemplate their potential solitary existence, a 21st century exigence for others.

What about the reverse situation though? How does a broadcaster know if the message is being received? I cannot know, will never know. My voice might just echo through eternity only to fall on deaf ears. Dead ears. The last human voice raising a cry of protestation that no one will ever hear.

Frayed nerves caused my hands to tremble as I reached for the controls below me. I felt ragged, broken by hours of horror and terrible unknowing; the gnawing pain deep within that ravaged my guts. I looked once more to reassure myself that the beacon wasn't active, that the incessant ringing I heard was just a lingering auditory phantom. The lights were still dark, the gauges at zero. With one hand, I toggled the mute.

"Sorry about that, folks", I began, staring over the top of the mic hanging before me. "That beacon was driving me nuts." I paused, one heartbeat, two, three. A rookie's mistake. I had seized up, unsure what to do next. Panicked, I closed my eyes. Feeling the wind on my face as my toes inched over the edge, I continued.

"I wish I had broken in on the emergency signal with good news… or any news for that matter. But the national feed went dark a few hours ago. This beacon is automated. Someone switched it on in Washington, but the message hasn't changed all night. Phone lines are dead, half the forest is on fire, and I haven't had a decent song request in hours." The joke fell flat. They always seem to when nobody's around to laugh. Who am I kidding, anyway? Just some madman atop a mountain, talking to the voices in his head.

"Maybe this is God's Wrath." Like a shot the words began flying out of my mouth before I could stop them. "Maybe it's aliens. Could be a violent outburst from Mother Nature. I don't have a clue, no one does. It's karmic retribution, the second flood; it's time for the human race to pay the fucking piper. Maybe this is Hell on Earth and those of you who can hear my voice are paying for your sins. I know I'm going to," I said, hearing my voice crack. Again, my hands trembled violently, but I didn't want to look down to steady them. Blood is so difficult to clean off your hands.

"So, what do we do now?" I asked no one in particular. "Beg for forgiveness? Pray to the saints? People have been doing that for centuries saying it gives them inner peace and salvation. I've tried it tonight, and I bet all of you have, too. Anyone get a goddamn response yet?" I screamed, banging the table and causing all the needles on the control monitors to execute synchronized jumps.

"We are in this warring, bloody Purgatory. Yet there is no peace on the other side, no beautiful white clouds waiting for our asses to sit upon them. No one's coming to help you and me. No Savior, no Salvation to be had in these fucking parts. I know, you damned listeners, because I've been watching from up on high and have yet to see a Single Fucking Sign!"

"I've fought and screamed, railed at what I've been called to witness. We've lost love, killed, and been reduced to base, animalistic survival... and for what? What do we have to hope for, to live for?" I paused, winded.

"Silence my friends. Nothingness. The sweet blackness of Nirvana. Oblivion may be all that's left to ease these pains that won't go away. It can be yours, if you aren't afraid of committing one final sin." At some point during my monologue I had picked it up again. It felt lighter somehow, now unburdened of its lethal ordinance. My crimson slicked palm stuck to the grip as I watched my finger curl from the guard to the trigger. *A last sin to perform, if I could finally decide to step off the edge.* "But first, a final confession."

...

The repetitive, bleating alarm slowly pushed away the beautiful, blissful haze in which I found myself swimming. I felt around blindly for the source. My semi-aware self found the bedside clock, and I began to smack every button atop it that my wooden, unresponsive fingers could touch. The noise stopped, and I felt myself begin to slide back into the wonderful fog of unconsciousness.

It began anew, and this time an inner rage began to build. A bit of logical thought somewhere in my mind cursed for choosing to collapse into bed in a drugged stupor the night before without checking its settings. A second dominant voice, the id of the moment, told the first to fuck off. I grabbed the clock and pulled, tossing it across the room where it made a satisfying slam against the wall.

The sound repeated, drawing me into total reality this time. I sat up, but my head felt too heavy for my body and I collapsed into sweat laden sheets. Blinking a few times, the ceiling came into focus. Normally upon waking I would be greeted by the blackness of night, lit only by a lamppost outside my second story apartment. Instead, brilliant beams of afternoon sunlight radiated across the popcorn decorated space, creating a textured world of light and shadow. My dick was swollen, I realized, my bladder full. Reaching beside me I could only feel the cool side of the bed, meaning the woman with purple highlights dropping LSD at the club last night hadn't come home with me... perhaps another reason for the painful swelling. Or maybe it was just the bladder.

The world had finished spinning, so I threw my legs over the side to stand. My mouth was dry and tasted bitter, but my now dexterous hands soon found a half-smoked cigarette in the bedside ash tray. One of these days I would forget to set it there before sleeping and set my stoned ass on fire, a smoker's version of a Viking funeral. I brought it to my lips, enjoying the sweet stale nicotine taste. Continuing to suck on it, my feet guided me to the bathroom where I took care of the other morning issue. As I began to piss, I felt for the lighter in my jeans. *Shit, I must have really been fucked up. Didn't even take my pants off last night.* I lit it, then took a drag. Bladder empty, lungs full of smoke. Today was a good day, even if I was pissed off to be awake for it.

A vibrating sensation started in my pocket, followed by a deep bass solo. A smooth and sultry ringtone, just like the Rabbit herself. I smiled at myself in the mirror before fishing the smartphone out to answer it.

"Hey beautiful, what's happening?" I asked.

"Those are some pretty words coming from you, Charlie," the full, deep, radio perfect voice on the other end of the line replied. "Rod said the last time he called you in the afternoon you tore his face off."

"It'd be a crying shame to hurt a beautiful face like yours, darling. Besides, I'm only civil to people I actually like."

"You only like me, Madman?" She sounded wounded, hurt. I could see her beautiful red lips forming a mock pout.

"You know you're the only lady for me, Jessica," I replied. "But I know when I am being played. What do you want?" She snickered, an uncontrollable habit she found distasteful, yet one I loved causing. The line went quiet, and I knew she was struggling to stop laughing.

"I need you to come in for me," she began. "I know it's the start of your week off," she continued, cutting off my immediate protestation, "but Rod was able to get backstage passes to the Springsteen concert tonight. I'm going to go live from the arena, and I need someone back at the station to watch the dials. I need you, Charlie," she said slowly for effect. I was being played for a sucker, but I didn't care. I knew she loved The Boss. "I'll make it up to you."

"You better," I replied. "Just let me put my dick back and I'll be over to make your day."

"If that's your idea of a pickup line, Madman, you are terrible." She laughed again with an indignant snort. "Kisses." I could hear the sound of a blown kiss over the line as she used her radio sign off before hanging up.

...

As my twenty-year-old sedan crested the top of the mountain, I saw the radio station glistening in the late afternoon sun. The once white exterior walls were stripped by the harsh Northeastern winters. The shabbiness continued to the massive tower that sat right behind the small one-story structure; the once brightly painted metal was peeling and rusting in a number of places. The giant neon letters that ran vertically down the piping had worked at one point, no longer functioned. Rod had promised to fix all these problems when he took over managing the station two years ago, but he had yet to do much other than make our summer interns wash windows.

WJPS is a shithole, I thought, *but it's my shithole.*

I had just finished parking when she flew through the grimy front doors looking like a million bucks. Some radio personalities acknowledged that it was a job and didn't care about content. Others have personas on air in the hopes to draw in listeners. Jessica Rabbit was a rare broadcaster because she genuinely enjoyed the music. WJPS was a classic rock station, and the Rabbit strutted out of that station looking like she was a backup dancer in a Poison music video.

The long blonde hair was always permed, the curled strands bouncing as she moved. Golden locks framed her smooth, creamy face perfectly. Light green eyes shone through thick, black mascara, a beautiful contrast to her full, rouged lips. She wasn't a thin woman; her body curved like the models of the past, before anorexia and starvation became the norm. She wore a mixture of spandex and leopard print with a jean jacket and skirt combination that expertly hid yet also accentuated every peak and valley of her body. I watched her sashay up to me in tall black heels, eyes sparkling to match a killer smile.

"I got you all set up in there, Charlie." She said, kissing my

95

cheek. "I owe you one," she whispered in my ear. Rabbit leaned back, remoistening her lips from the contact. *I am such a sucker for a pretty woman.* I still didn't care.

"Enjoy the peace and quiet of the station." With a wink and wry grin, she walked away. Staring at her from that angle, it took my brain a few moments to process the meaning of what she had said.

"Peace and quiet. What do you mean? Where's Rod?" The doors crashed again, and as I turned; my mistake was finally clear.

Rod was also stuck in the 80's, but for every bit Jessica sparkled, he oozed sleaze. Black hair poorly dyed was slicked straight back with what appeared to be a hundred ounces of product. Rod was decked out in a faux vintage black AC/DC shirt that he likely bought at Hot Topic a month ago. He wore hip hugging jeans, and I swear to God he stuffed a tube sock down the front of them. The most unappealing aspect was his long, waxed mustache that read more as Ron Jeremy then it did Tom Selleck. Below the facial hair nightmare Rod wore a mile wide grin. He had fucked me, and we both knew it.

Without warning, Rod flipped a set of keys towards me. I lurched to grab them, trying not to look like a total fool. I half succeeded. "Keep the place running, and clean the bathroom while you're at it. We'll be doing the live report between 9 and 10. Don't screw up again, Charlie," he said, all while getting into the driver's side of the van. Without leaving an opening for rebuttal he jumped in, started the vehicle, and took off. I was left cooling my heels as he drove off with the hottest woman in town. There was only one thing that came to my mind at a time like this.

"Fuck me. I need a hit."

...

Running the station solo is a tedious and boring prospect. When working the weekends there would usually be another person or two here with me, so sharing some conversation, a cigarette, or even a beer or two wasn't out of the question. On a weekday evening Rod and Jessica should be here, and, barring his absence, one of the weekend engineers would be called in to cover. He hadn't done so, a further sign of the good fucking he had given me. Over the last hour I had watched the city below, lights winking on like stars coming out on a clear night. It was beautiful. The sun had finally set beyond the mountain range, and I could see the network of cars, homes, and streets laid out below me. Hell, one or two of them might even be listening to my voice right now.

That'll do the trick, I realized. Listener calls were always entertaining. On the weekends I would field calls from drunks, addicts, and anyone else high on sex and drugs that needed some rock n' roll to complete the trifecta. I double checked the computer and saw that we were nearly at the end of our half hour block of back-to-back rock. Making sure my preset sound cues were loaded, I watched the final guitar note fade before cueing up the mic before me.

"Gotta love that BTO, right? I know I love to work at nothing all day. This is Charlie the Madman..." I pressed the SFX board and the obnoxious sounds of crazy laughter and explosions drifted across the airwaves. "Madison, and I am standing in for Jessica Rabbit tonight. She'll be coming to you all live from backstage with the Boss himself, but for the next hour or so it's just you, me, and great tunes. Give me a call, the lines are wide open." I played the commercial break, hoping the bait would reel in something interesting. Two thirds of the way through an ad for discount car washes, the call waiting button began to blink. I debated screening it for a moment; it's station policy. That job was usually done by the guy in the booth, though. *Fuck it,* I thought. *Hopefully this asshole swears on air and Rod gets hit with a steep FCC penalty.* The final commercial about Crazy Ed's Fireworks Warehouse ended, and I toggled my mic and the phone line live.

"Hello, you are live on WJPS the Spark. Speak to the Madman, brother," I said, silently hoping it was a man on the other end of the line.

"Hello, hello?" The voice was male, soft spoken, with just a hint of echo. Swearing at myself for not checking the audio levels, I increased the gain.

"Yes man, you are on the air with Charlie. Hit me."

"Have you heard about the park yet?" I felt the frown form on my face. They never ask questions; usually you give an idiot an open forum and they'll talk about nothing for hours. *Dead air, moron.*

"What's going down out there? Tell the Madman what's happening."

"There's something in the park. I think it's killing, eating." A cold shiver ran down my spine. His words had been broken, muffled. I must be mistaken.

"Speak up, my man. The Spark wants to hear your story."

"It's like a bear, or dog." He continued as if he hadn't heard me. "But bigger. The eyes weren't human, but it was... or might once have been. I saw it take a child in one massive paw, then it... The blood..." he trailed off, attempting to stifle tears. My hand hovered over the kill switch. I was being fucked with, but this was more interesting than sitting in the studio by myself.

"Sure, and you called a radio station before the police. Ok, I'll bite. What are you advertising? I'll give you ten seconds of free air to pitch your movie or YouTube channel, or whatever. Clock's ticking."

"I already called; they're on their way. But they won't make it. They can't help me. It tore the kid in two before ripping out the throats of the two men who went to save him. I wanted to let everyone know. Stay out of the south side park." He stopped suddenly. Sounds of heavy breathing and scuffling came across the receiver. I knew I should hit the dump button, but there was something in what he said, the panicked trembling of his voice or the terror he inspired that had me gripped. I had to see how far he would push it. A new noise joined the rustling, an animalistic breathing, padded steps that stalked the other end of the line. A low growl.

"Please God, make it go away. Can you hear it?" he asked me, voice dropping even lower. "It's right outside my car." The noises slowly disappeared and a sigh of relief echoed over the line. I realized I had been holding my breath.

"Excellent performance bro," I said, toggling the applause SFX.

"SHUT UP!" he screamed in a hushed manner, more pleading than demanding. The muffled sounds returned, then silence. "Oh my God, there's more than one." Then he began to scream.

I toggled the dump button. "Sorry about that everyone. It seems the Madman brings out all the local crazies. Wicked good sound effects, though, right? Too bad I had to cut the call off before he could give us the name of his slasher flick. I didn't get a request out of him, either. But no worries, ol' Charlie has just the thing. This one goes out to you, Mr. Victim." The vamped monologue gave me enough time to cue up the perfect song. The iconic piano intro began as I heard the first siren. For some reason, I felt drawn to the window.

The south side park was only a mile or two from the station, and from atop the mountain the city was spread out before me like a map. In the distance I could see flashing lights, a lot of them, outside of where I estimated the entrance of the park was. Behind me, Warren began to sing about Lee Ho Fook's beef chow mein. As he started in with his trademark howl to the moon, I heard a gunshot. Then another. And another.

• • •

The station had a scanner in the booth tuned to the generic dispatch channels for police and fire. Since WJPS was such a small station it was useful in keeping us up to date on road hazards as well as news stories. I paused long enough to add another half hour's worth of audio content to the live feed before throwing open the door to the audio engineering room. Full of anticipation and a hint of dread, I flipped on the switch and waited as the receiver came on, a large red 01 coming to life on its LED screen.

"Dispatch, shots fired, repeat, shots fired." The man's voice was even, unfazed by whatever shitstorm he found himself in.

"Repeat and identify, possible 10-60," a second voice replied.

"Car 59, badge 7642, we are 10-23, responding to calls for backup at 1147 East Cheney Lane. 10-4 on that 10-60. I've got two squad cars, 17 and 38, but no sign of the officers. There is gunfire in the area." The officer clicked off. He was at the park but not the first responder.

"7642, reports of a possible 10-80?" The voice raised slightly at the end of the phrase, making this indecipherable string of numbers a question.

"Negative, dispatch, my partner…" he paused, the comm left open. I could hear a whispered conversation. "Check dispatch, we appear to be alone. Request additional backup."

"En route, 7642. 10-84 five minutes."

"Clear dispatch. We…"

"What the fuck?" A new voice asked. The line from the park abruptly went dead.

"10-9, 7642. Please repeat." The scanner was silent for several agonizing moments as red numbers scrolled across the LED screen in quick succession. There was a slight crackle as the line opened again and then loud, concussive shots blared from the small speaker.

"DISPATCH SHOTS FIRED SHOTS FIRED!" Badge 7642 screamed. The passive demeanor was gone, replaced by raw terror. The world around him was a cacophony of sounds: some gunshots, shouts from a partner, and a terrible shrieking I couldn't identify. "We are under attack by, what the fuck is that? Where's the goddamn backup!" he screamed, and again the line went dead.

"10-84 two minutes, 7642." Dispatch seemed unnerved.

"Fuck two minutes. Officer down. Get them here right the FUCK NOW!" The shrieks were louder, more defined. There were howls... like the ones I had heard from the caller.

"10-4, 7642. Please update."

"He's dead goddamnit, that thing, it... Oh my god, there's dozens of them." The line stayed open this time. He began to scream incoherently as he discharged the pistol again and again. All around the shrieks and howls crescendoed then blended together. With each round one of the yips seemed to falter but did not stop.

"Shit, shit, shit," he mumbled to himself, and I could hear a metallic fumbling. Perhaps he was attempting to reload. Then a new noise, one that sounded salivary and deadly. Like the opening of a giant maw. Something crunched, and he screamed the painful wailing of a dying thing. More crunching joined the first as the clear sounds of a feast were heard. After several gut-wrenching moments, they stopped to howl once more in unison. I turned the scanner off, my hands trembling. *What the fuck was going on? The caller may have been a prank, but what was this?* I collapsed in the engineer's chair, rolling slowly across the tiled floor. I couldn't get the sound of that howl out of my head.

Then I realized I wasn't imagining the sound. The horrific cacophony of these beasts yipping as one continued. The scanner was no longer on, I was hearing the howl echo in the valley below. Staring out the window, the prominence of the full moon struck me as it rose above the horizon.

...

I made it back into the studio just in time to hear the office phone start ringing. Wiping the vomit from my mouth, I stumbled into the broadcast room. The public call-in lines were silent; one of the private business lines was lit up. I checked to make sure the programming I had added was still going out On Air, then hurried to answer.

"Charlie, what's going on?" Jessica's voice was tense, edgy. "We were listening to the station backstage. I heard that creepy caller, then you dumped a half hour of blind audio."

"I'm not sure," I replied, steadying my shaking voice. "It doesn't seem like a crank, though. Something's happening out there tonight Jess. They're... hunting."

"What the hell are you talking about, Madman?" Her tone was insulting to lighten the mood but instead came off as a panicked joke.

"The police scanner has been wailing nonstop. Shit is going down in the park, like the fucking purge or something. I think there are a lot of them out there." I paused, attempting to gauge her mood. "How are things at the Arena?"

"Curtain has been delayed. It's quiet here; everyone seems to be checking their phones. I've never been at a concert this silent before. It's weird."

"They haven't said anything about problems on that side of the city. Things will be fine."

"I hope so." Jessica sounded lost. That bothered me, more than I would have thought.

"Besides, this is Rod's big moment. He'd love to protect you, the Miami Vice wannabe." She tittered, nerves stealing away the trademark laughter. The jab hadn't improved her mood as I had hoped.

"I haven't seen him in awhile. He wandered off after you set the long track list. Probably going to call and bitch at you for not breaking in on the rock block enough times." I checked my phone reflexively at the mention of contact. No missed calls, no texts. "Kinda lonely backstage now."

"You'll. Be. Fine." I paused after each word for emphasis in a vain attempt to comfort her across the phone line.

"I know," she conceded. "Thanks Charlie, I'll let you know when" a multitude of surprised screams on Jessica's end drowned out the rest of her sentence.

"Jessica, what the fuck is going on. Jessica? Jessica!" I screamed several times at the receiver, hearing only chaos in response. Though it felt like hours, the voices quickly faded out.

"We lost power Charlie, the place is dark. People are freaked out."

"Good, I thought something happened. Be sure to stay…"

"Wait a minute," Jessica interrupted. "There's something. I can't quite see it in the crowd." She paused, staring out into what I imagined to be a field of cell phones being used as flashlights. Since she went silent, it became easier to hear the crowd. They seemed anxious, but there was something else I could hear as well. A rumble, throaty and deep. It was that growl. In the distance a woman screamed. More followed.

"Jessica, get the fuck out, now! Run, goddamnit."

"Charlie, someone's hurt. There are people out there; I think they're being attacked."

"It's those things. Run, Jessica."

"Ohmygodohmygodohmygod." I could hear her running amidst the backdrop of unending screams and howls. "Charlie, they're everywhere. What the hell are these things?" Jessica screamed then, and I heard the phone hit the ground. Jaws snapped on her end. Then the phone went dead.

I called back. Busy signal. I redialed, sweaty hands fumbling at the phone. Still busy. Third time. It began to ring, and my breath caught in my throat. Body quaking, I listened as the line rang once. Twice. On the third ring, the line connected. Then three loud tones rang out from the receiver in my hand.

"We're sorry, this service has been temporarily disabled. Please wait a few moments and try again." The automated monotone then disconnected the call, and I was left listening to the dial tone. A flat line. Dead Air. I screamed, slamming my fists against the table. The rage, unquenched by this sudden outburst instead percolated in the pit of my stomach. I felt my quivering body sink to floor as the tears began to fall.

...

The Arena is across the city. The thought suddenly occurred to me. Their voices had been in the room, providing an intimate disclosure of their terrifying experience. Geographically speaking, however, the two locations were miles apart. *What the fuck is really going on?*

Instinctively I returned to the glass walled broadcast room. After grabbing the remote, I watched as the TV began to glow; the set emitting an accompanying whine as the tubes heated up. *TVs don't use tubes anymore, idiot.* If this was a citywide nightmare, someone else was watching. They are always watching these days; even the most inane occurrence made headline news. People were dying below me… surely I wasn't the only voyeur to have a front row seat to the madness.

The set came on preset to the local news; again, a further source of information the station could pass on in its broadcast. But the local anchors weren't there. It seemed the feed was being superseded by national coverage. In a giant studio overlooking Manhattan, broadcasters were discussing the breaking news in the City. The scrolling text suggested a large scale, metropolitan attack. Common consensus agreed a massive terrorist cell had been activated in response to recent political changes in the Middle East. *NYC is hundreds of miles from here. Surely this isn't...* My train of thought was interrupted as the scene abruptly changed, shifting from a sterile and unassuming interior to a chaotic exterior shot. They had gone live to Times Square, where a beautiful young Latina focused on making an eyewitness statement of the pandemonium around her.

The square was packed with bustling people and there was a note of tension in the mob. It had the desire to surge but seemed unsure of where to go. The crowd bumped into each other like waves crashing against the shore. It seemed ready to break at any moment. The young woman, however, never broke eye contact with the camera. She had an air of nervous excitement about her, the bloodhound nature of a reporter taking over. The situation felt monumental, and it was evident that she wanted to be on the front lines of the story.

Without warning, the levee broke and the crowd surged as one. The terrified cries of hundreds drowned out her report, and like one caught out in a rising storm she turned slightly, watching the oncoming tempest. The crew had sequestered themselves against a corner of a building, and their location served its purpose well. Most of the screaming New Yorkers ran past them, and with her back against the wall she was safe from being swept up by the mob. The cameraman was perfectly positioned to capture the restrained fear upon her face and the unbridled terror in the runners on the sidewalk beside her.

In moments the sound balanced out, and the young woman returned to the camera, her brown eyes sparkling with excitement. She kept repeating to the talking heads in the studio that she had no clue what was causing this, but that as soon as the crowd cleared out the crew would be on their way into the square to investigate. I tuned out the prattle, instead finding myself absorbed in the horror behind her. People were trampled, knocked over, punched. Then one ran by with blood on his shirt, then a woman with a head wound. Like passing trees in a car, they flew by; giving only a glimpse of what might be the cause of this mass panic.

I saw it then, for just a split second. A dark form amongst the crowd, stalking them. It was just a blur at first. Then a second, a third. A teenage boy was knocked to the ground across the street, and for a split second as the crowd parted I saw the shadow crouching over him, a hairy, inhuman beast. Then it was gone, as the sea of people closed. Red eyes seemed to appear interspersed throughout the crowd. In unison they turned toward the camera, and I stifled a scream. I feared my cry might cause their gaze to fall on me.

A form moved through the crowd, dividing people in its unerring path to the alley. The woman and the crew seemed oblivious to their current peril. I watched as it silently stalked her. The thing was a head taller than any human around it, yet it seemed to slink across the ground like a prowling beast. The face was drawn into a long muzzle that stretched from between the narrow, ruby colored eyes. Canine teeth rested upon saliva covered jowls, and a dog's nose twitched at the scent of its prey. The body was lean and muscular. Though built like a human it seemed to find the upright, bipedal motion unnatural. Long, yellowed talons tipped its fingers, blood running from the oversized human paws. The blood slicked its entire body, I realized. The dark fur was matted by it, running up and down its arms. A huge trail ran from its muzzle down its long legs. It reached the sidewalk before the camera crew realized it was there.

With one massive hand the beast tore into her soft, fleshy abdomen, choking off a scream. The claws twisted in her guts and, finding purchase inside her, lifted the hyperventilating woman off her feet. Its long jaws opened, and the microphone that she awkwardly had clenched in her hand picked up the wet smacking that emanated from within its crimson stained mouth. With a sickening crunch, it slammed her small body against the wall, whiplashing her against the concrete. I prayed she lost consciousness. Displaying unbelievable quickness, the beast's head turned and tore through her neck before the head had a chance to loll back. I watched horrified as the gore covered thing lapped up the arterial spray, using it to wash down the mangled flesh it had already chewed. The entire attack had taken less than two seconds.

Perhaps it was because of this suddenness the cameraman never changed focus on his subject. Maybe it was professional instinct. Yet as the blood covered beast dropped the once gorgeous beat reporter to the ground where her nearly severed neck broke upon impact; he finally realized the situation he was in. The camera fell, and the sounds of fast footfalls against the blood slicked pavement echoed from the still live microphone. The beast, incensed by fleeing prey, took off after him.

At this point the feed returned back to the newsroom. One of the anchors appeared to have fainted and was being attended to by the crew. Another was vomiting uncontrollably behind the desk. My recently agitated guts sympathized, and I turned away from the purging of her stomach to try and keep from doing the same. *This goes beyond our little town*, I realized. This is something much bigger, much worse than I could have ever imagined. Returning to the window I could see fires below, helicopters circling some of the larger ones. Sirens echoed, unceasing wails of the horrors below. The scanner continued to broadcast nonstop. Looking back at the TV, the attack was being replayed. They had already censored the reporter's violent death and were showing it again and again. It had become clear this wasn't a coordinated attack due to the sheer scale of the violence. This was an outbreak, a contagion; like some tsunami of horrific nightmares that swamped over Earth. Everywhere these beasts infected the cities, invaded homes, nightclubs, and offices. America's blood ran in the streets knee deep. All I could do was watch it unfold.

I remembered the needle I had in my pocket. Usually I avoided the harder stuff, stuck to pot, LSD... maybe a little X.

Needles, though, I shied away from. As slaying after slaying played out on the screen, I found myself playing with the hypodermic. I unconsciously rolled it in my left hand, twiddling it like a pen across my fingers. The silver tip glistened in the light, shining like a beacon of hope. The dream of forgetfulness, the relief of being numb would lead to the salvation of escape. Watching as someone else's hands went through the motion of finding a spoon, liquefying the stuff, filling the needle... *It must be some junkie. I'm watching a movie. This isn't me.*

Realization struck as the tourniquet tightened, followed by the needle poking through skin, my arm tensing as the vein was struck solidly. Did I want to do this? The pain of what I had seen and heard was excruciating, but to lose myself in search of some drug addled Nirvana? I looked away from the syringe casting my gaze across the room where it fell upon a poster advertising the station. In an imitation of old album covers the fonts were big and bright, casting rainbow shadows across the background. Photoshopped terribly astride a majestic white horse, her hair blowing in a fake wind, was the Rabbit. *Jessica.*

It burned suddenly, all over. My flesh crawled beneath the surface, and I felt my heart begin to race. Temple's throbbing, I looked down to see that I had depressed the plunger. Vision wavering like heat upon asphalt, I removed the surgical tubing before sinking lower in the chair. For the first time in hours, life felt comfortably numb.

...

The world was bright. Then dark. Then bright once more. The source of illumination vibrated, flickering. Then it all plunged into darkness. A long, monotonous drone rang through my ears, lifting me from sleep. *My alarm.* I swam up through the black pit, searching for consciousness. *It's all a dream.* The thought spurred me onward though I wasn't sure why. Struggling against a strong force that wanted to drown me, I fought hard, my arms spinning wildly until I broke the surface.

The tile was cold, the word still black. No, not completely. Soft red lighting made the room shadowy, and some indirect white light flooded from under the door. Somewhere a voice spoke. Slowly I moved my hands to the sides to push myself off the floor. Grabbing the console to keep from falling, I maintained an upright position. *It's not a dream, I'm still in Hell.*

The studio was lit by emergency lights, and the backup generator WJPS had for outages was rumbling down the hall. It would keep us broadcasting for hours, giving updates to the powerless and frightened people below. Assuming someone sober was at the controls. A sonorous voice echoed from the broadcast; its timbre soft yet forceful. With halting steps and wobbling legs, I moved slowly into the other room.

No one sat in the chair, the microphones sat with no one to speak through them. Yet the voice persisted, an invisible specter warning of possible dangers. "Stay in your homes," it suggested. "You will be informed of important developments as they arise," the apparition reassured. With a glance over my shoulder, I saw the needles rise and bounce as the phantom continued. "Alert your local fire and police of any emergencies." These words were being broadcast over the airwaves and weren't a side effect of impure heroin.

Noticing an unusual red light in one of the audio towers, I stumbled over to investigate. A small device labeled emergency broadcast beacon was on and active. These units had become standard operating equipment after 9/11, allowing the government to broadcast important warnings all across the country in the event of a large-scale incident. This was the first time I had ever seen it active. The message repeated after forty seconds or so; I listened to it several times to be sure I understood its words. It was a canned, prerecorded message with no solid information or news. Near the end, the voice promised periodic updates and encouraged continuous listening of this broadcasting station. *Probably the largest audience WJPS has ever had on a weekday night.*

I went to the window to connect with some other form of human life. Outside, the city was dark. Power outage must have affected the whole city. The city was glowing in the light of several massive fires, visible even up here in the peeling concrete tower. Otherwise the world was dark, with the exception of the massive full moon. I gazed into it, feeling akin to the celestial body. It, much like myself, was powerless to affect what we saw below. We could only watch the devastation as it occurred.

Movement in my periphery brought me out of the drug influenced reverie. Something was out there, and it was close. The parking lot, perhaps. Moving this direction. Adrenaline spiking, I ducked below the window, hugging the exterior wall as my heart raced. I heard the beast before I saw it. Like some massive dog it panted, the grating mouth breathing approached my position. On the spotless tile floor, I saw its outline etched in moonlight. The creature towered above the sill; its hairy bulk softened by back lighting. The panting stopped suddenly as the shadow beast cocked its head. It began to sniff like a bloodhound, the elongated nose becoming prominent then disappearing into the shadowed outline once more as it turned its head toward me. Stomach acid churning, I covered my mouth with both hands to muffle my own breathing. At any moment I expected the thing to crash through the glass, reach down, and pull me through the shards so that it could feast upon my organs. Again and again, I thought of the beautiful reporter. Then the hellhound stopped, turning once more to reveal its shadowed muzzle. I jumped, biting my tongue not to scream as it raised its furry face and howled. The solitary yip was soon answered by others. Then the outline was gone, the floor once more a perfect square of full moon light.

I sat there in my own puddle of piss for several minutes, straining my ears to assure myself that nothing was there. *I need a weapon.* With slow and deliberate action, I crawled across the floor, taking care to avoid the sightlines of the various windows. Once into the dark corridor I shuffled along briskly, trying not to contemplate a visceral death at the hands of these unholy beasts.

...

The bottle rattled items on the console as I set it down too hard, the brown, semi-transparent contents threatening to spill across the top of the equipment. The clatter caused me to wince. I bit back the curse forming in my lips, instead glancing nervously in the direction of the window. Instinctively my hand tightened around the unfamiliar grip of the revolver. In darkest silence, I waited to see if the nightmares outside had heard the noise. One heartbeat, two. There was no sound other than the monotonous repetition of the government broadcast in the background. After it pumped a hundred times, I let out the breath I had been holding and laid the gun back down.

It was more of a weapon than I could have hoped for, though given how the officers had fared it was likely as useless as anything improvised. Rummaging through Rod's desk I had found the piece loaded with six bullets. I turned and picked up the vintage bottle of whiskey, watching the air bubbles burp inside the crystal holder as I took several long swigs. It was nearly gone, another supply I had swiped from my rat bastard boss. *At least he had proved useful in one thing.*

The ringing broke the near silence of the studio like a gunshot, its peal echoing throughout the room. *Fuckfuckfuckfuckfuck.* In blind panic I knocked the landline off the desk. It fell to the floor in a clatter, the handset skipping a short distance away. Grabbing the revolver once more, I listened for ominous growls.

"Charlie, are you there?" The question was distant, the voice that queried it barely perceptible. It wasn't real. Just a side effect of the drugs and booze, a bad mix. Paranoia wasn't helping either.

"Charlie, please answer. I. need. help." A woman, I decided. The voice weak, pained. *Jessica.* I scrambled across the floor, reaching for the receiver.

"Jessica? Jessica, answer me." The line was all static, but I could make out some labored breathing. Heart pounding so hard it threatened to burst from my chest, I cried out over and over. "Jessica, say something, please God. Anything."

"I'm alone Charlie. It's dark and cold. I think I hear them." Her sultry radio voice strained as she fought to utter each syllable.

"What happened? Are you alright; are you safe?"

"I can hear them. I've listened to them eating for hours Charlie. But they've stopped. I think they're looking for more people. For me. We're just food to them."

"Are you still in the Arena? Where are you?" In a panic, I tried to decide whether or not I could run to my car without them getting me, if I could get to her in time.

"I'm bleeding. A lot. It hurts." She moaned softly, stifling the pain. "He left me here," she continued, switching subjects. "So. Alone. No one wants to die alone."

"Stop that," I pleaded. "Don't you dare, goddamnit, don't you fucking dare!"

"I…. I just needed to hear someone else. You. were. it. Thank you, Charlie."

"No, God, nonono." Hot tears stained my face. "I thought I lost you already. I can't go through this again."

"You think you're a bad guy, Charlie, but you aren't. You've got a good heart. Never forget that."

"Please, Jessica, please stop."

"K…ki…kisses," she gasped. Then the Rabbit went silent. Through the earpiece I heard those distinctive snarls approach. The sounds got closer and louder. *Please God, if you're there, stop this. Stop this whole Fucking Thing.* I hadn't prayed in years, but I did so now on the floor of the studio. *Save her. Protect her from Evil.* Sniffing became growling, then I heard a crunch. She screamed. Again. And again. And again.

With an inhuman wail I smashed the phone against the floor over and over before collapsing in a heap. Sobbing, I rocked myself to sleep.

The rustling woke me from a mindless reverie. It felt like I had slept for months, years. A glance at my cell showed it had been less than an hour. Still no service. I discovered that I was laying in piles of plastic and metal, wires strewn about the place. *The phone,* I realized. That had happened. It was real. The noises down the hall continued... a shuffling, metal on metal perhaps. I was alone. It could only be

THEM. My body tensed like a taut cord, more awake than if I had taken an upper. On my hands and knees I crawled slowly to the door, avoiding the setting moonlight that still radiated through the windows. Something was here, maybe even in the station. Though terrified earlier, some bit of cognition had implored me to lock the doors with the keys I had found in Ron's office. Now I was glad I had, though I was not assured of the security of the padlocked chain I now heard clanking against the crash bar. The noises were caused by something beyond the front doors.

Reaching the hallway, I turned to look at the doors. The glass was frosted, but a human like form stood silhouetted by the pale moon. The head was down, its attention focused on the doors. It rattled them once more then stopped. The form swiveled, looking to see if it had been overheard. I paused, confused by the creature's skillful approach to getting inside rather than smashing its way through. Slowly, I approached the front foyer.

It crouched now in an attempt to conceal itself by hugging the door. The thing fumbled some more. Then the unmistakable sound of a key rattling within the lock. It wasn't one of those things; it was human. And someone who worked at the station, no less. Moving more swiftly now, I reached the doors just as I heard the key click within the lock. The doors pried open about two feet before the chain caught, preventing them from moving any further. There, standing before me, was Rod.

My boss was drenched in sweat. His jacket was torn in several places, and parts of his body were slicked in blood. Locking eyes with me, Rod looked like a mouse that has discovered itself locked in the aquarium with a snake. He radiated fear, so much so that he quivered. As the gaze continued, his countenance changed from terror to recognition, then to hope. With one arm wedged in the door in an attempt to enter through the narrow gap, he reached for me, his groping fingers inches from my crouched form.

"Charlie, oh my god, Charlie. Let me in, quick. I saw them on the drive up here; they're not far behind." His speech was rapid, pleading. Without waiting for my response, he continued to grope for me in some effort for contact with another human being.

"Where's Jessica?" I asked, surprised at the calm in my voice. I slowly rose to stand tall in front of the station manager.

"I don't know, man, one minute she was beside me and the next... fuck, Jesus let me in and we can talk about it Charlie."

"You left her," I said flatly. A statement, not an accusation. His eyes grew wide with a wild panic.

"No man, she was with me. We were running to the van and... all the people. She was trampled. I tried to turn back for her, but she was gone. For the love of God let me in."

"She called me, just a little while ago." Rod paused, the fear for his life abated by my words. "Jessica lay there as those things surrounded her. She listened to them stalk her as she lay there helpless. Because of you." I watched his eyes mist, his lip tremble.

Then the vulnerability disappeared as he became hardened against the accusations I hurled at him.

"You listen to me, you little shit. This is my goddamn station and I'll be damned if some piss-ant doesn't let me into it. I made it through a fucking war zone and I will not die by these fucking beasts you goddamned junkie. So you let me in right the fuck now, Charlie." His voice never rose above a whisper, but it was full of violence and demanded respect. I refused to give it to him.

"Fuck you, Rod. Go to hell. You left her, ran off to save your own goddamn neck. Left her to die, and I... I listened. Unable to do anything about it. And you ran from that." My vision blurred as the memories of her last, soft, pain-filled words came across the phone. How horrific it must have been for her, in those last dark moments.

I never saw him move. With blinding speed Rod swiped at me, managing to grab me by the collar and drag me towards him. His teeth were bared like a rabid dog as he pulled me close, his intentions violent.

CRACK.

The lightning strike hit, and I felt the strong hand relax just a bit, before tightening again.

CRACK.

Another bolt and Rod's mouth twisted.

CRACK. CRACK. CRACK.

Three more times the hammer struck, and an acrid smell reached my nose. Looking down beyond his outstretched hand the revolver smoked, and directly in front of it I saw a number of roses blooming across the AC/DC t-shirt.

Then the howls began. Behind him, to the sides, everywhere. I could hear them running, loping across the parking lot, incensed by the stench of blood in the air. Rod and I locked eyes once more, and

I could see the fear growing within him. The terror. He struggled to get in past the chain but the once powerful motions were childlike by comparison. Rod discovered his inability to even make the doors budge. As the first beast arrived, I watched it tower over his frame, felt its hot breath cascade off his neck and hit me flush in the face. As its jaws opened wide and tore into him, I felt the slippery drool and coppery blood spatter my face.

Rod's grip redoubled on my shirt as the creature tore into his back. His eyes pleaded, but they were different now. He glanced down at the gun then back at me, a question. Begging. I nodded, bringing the revolver up slightly.

CRACK.

Rod groaned softly. Then his eyes grew wide with realization. Looking down, the dying man saw the last bullet had embedded itself in his left foot. More of those things approached, looking for ways to get at the warm meal. Rod reached out to me one last time.

I grabbed his hand and shoved. The weakened man put up no resistance, instead tumbling easily into the fury of claws and teeth behind him. The beasts paid me no mind as I slowly closed the door, relocking it. Outside, Rod screamed for a long time. Even in death, he was one tough bastard. Wiping my brow, I cleared sweat, saliva, and blood from my face. I then discovered something unexpected. I was smiling.

...

"So that's the story, friends, of how the Madman went mad." I had expected strong emotion in the retelling, but instead I felt calm. Deathly still. "I'm tired of playing witness to it all. No more prayers." I paused, thinking. "No. One last prayer to whoever may be listening up above. God, make me the last one on Earth. I will no longer bear witness to the end of mankind. I've been an unworthy replacement for Job." I looked out the window one last time at the destruction that had been wrought. Everything I knew and loved had been destroyed throughout the course of the night. Devils hunted among us, tearing us apart. And I had helped. *Enjoyed it,* I realized with a start. Perhaps I was no better than those things, maybe none of us ever were. Like wild beasts we did nothing but prey upon each other; why in the end should our demise be any different?

"The sun will be up in a few hours. I'm not sure what kind of world will be left. A quieter one, I suppose. More peaceful. We'll all rot and Earth will grow around our bones. One giant cemetery for mankind. But I'm not going to see it. The Madman's got a one-way ticket to eternal blackness, and the train is leaving the station now." I turned to look behind me at the construction. It was crude but fitting. The emergency beacon had wedged tightly within the low rafters of the studio. I was not worried that it would break before I was finished. The bundle of cord was wrapped in a tight noose; a custom fit. The irony of using it to kill myself seemed appropriate; I just needed one last detail to set the mood perfectly.

"Before I go, I'd like to leave you all with one last thing. I've done this job a long time, and it only seems appropriate to spin one last disc before I go. A final turn on the table. This song needs no introduction. I hope you enjoy. This is Charlie 'The Madman' Madison signing off." A drum solo kicked in hard and fast. The needles jumped with the staccato snare; it was too loud. I didn't care. Dragging the chair back, I heard that Lenny Bruce wasn't afraid. Neither was I.

Standing on the chair's seat the noose was within easy reach. I tied it just a bit too high so that I was forced to stand on tiptoes to thread the needle's eye with my throat. It was snug, a tad uncomfortable. It would suffice. Closing my eyes, I began to headbang to the chorus. Everything was just fine. Perfect. On the edge of the cliff. Then I kicked the chair out.

Something was wrong. My body fell through the air as the knot slipped, cutting circulation. But my neck wasn't broken. I gasped, choking for breath. Instinctively my hands reached for the electric cable to pry myself loose as my vision blurred. Then Stipe's nonsensical rambling invaded my ears. It was clear for the first time, dreamlike and ethereal. Words beckoned, inviting me to that dark place. The end. All I had to do was let go and fall. My hands relaxed to my sides as the final refrain played, one last guitar solo fading out in the distance. The end of the world. Slowly everything faded to black.

A drum solo broke the Silence, killing my perfect ending. I had to know why. Opening my eyes, I saw colors swimming before me, bright luminescence floating in the air. All my listeners were here, their souls rocking out with me before departing. *I'm coming,* I tried to cry out. *I'm right behind you.* Forcing my eyes to focus I looked at the console once more. A single light blinked on the player. Repeat. The irony caused me to sputter and choke, the best laugh a hanged man could give the situation. As the world went dark, I felt that same strange feeling creep across my face. A smile.

POOKY

By Matthew Heslop

Saturday 22nd June 2024

I hesitate to write this for fear that nobody will believe me. I hardly believe it myself. I still wouldn't believe it if my house wasn't in ruins and there wasn't a dead person lying in there.

Last night my wife, two daughters and I were watching TV. My youngest daughter got up to look outside. She commented on how pretty the full moon looked then returned to the couch.

Not five minutes later she started complaining about not feeling well. She started complaining of feeling hot and itchy. That's when our German shepherd started barking at her. I tried to calm him, but nothing worked. Eventually, she just went to her room to lie down.

The dog followed her and as he did, I noticed the hair down his spine was standing up.

I figured I'd give my youngest daughter 10 minutes to get settled in bed, then I'd go down and check on her before going to bed myself.

Only a few minutes later, I heard the dog going ballistic at my daughter's bedroom door. I ran down to see what had caused the outburst. He was jumping and clawing at the door trying to get through it. I pulled him back and knocked on the door. Something in the room was crying or whimpering. I cracked the door open to see what she was doing, and that's when I saw it. There was a large wolf in the room. I swung the door open to pull her out of there but she was gone.

The wolf started growling at me and posturing, ready to lunge. I quickly retreated and pulled the door shut as the wolf leapt, hitting the door as it closed.

Claws ripped on the other side, trying to tear through the door. I held it with all my might and began screaming for my wife to grab something I could use to secure the door closed.

The dog was still going crazy barking at the bedroom door. The chaos of the two animals barking was disorienting and I wanted to get away from that door as quickly as possible.

I called to my oldest daughter to bring me my shotgun. She looked at me in shock, my request not registering with her yet. She was still trying to make sense of the large animal she could hear on the other side of her sister's bedroom door.

"Hey!" I yelled, "Wake up and go get my shotgun." She finally realized I was talking to her and ran upstairs to retrieve the shotgun I keep for home protection.

My wife returned with a length of nylon rope. I took it and quickly started tying two-bedroom doorknobs together.

"Where is she?" My wife's voice was strained and full of fear. The thoughts of our missing daughter terrified her. "I don't know; I thought she was in her room." I replied nervously.

My oldest daughter returned with my shotgun. I took it and quickly racked a round into the chamber. I turned and looked both of them in the eyes so I could make sure they understood what I was about to tell them.

"Go back upstairs and lock yourself in my bedroom. Grab the AR15 and don't open the door for anyone that isn't me."

I pulled the dog away from the door and handed his collar to my wife. She struggled to pull him upstairs with her.

As they ascended the stairs, I began searching the house for my youngest. She wasn't anywhere to be found.

The animal in her room had given up on the door, so I decided to take a peek inside again and do another scan for my daughter in case she was hiding in her closet or under the bed.

I quietly undid the rope securing her doorknob and cracked the door open. The wolf was sitting on her bed quietly watching the door. It raised its head as I opened the door more. "Psst," I whispered with no answer. "You in there?" I said a little louder, still no answer.

The wolf began to growl at me again. I raised the barrel of my shotgun in case the wolf made a move towards me. It noticed the gun and backed down a little, moving its head toward my daughter's favorite stuffed animal, nuzzling the plush creature with its nose. Something wasn't right about the situation and my heart said not to just kill this thing, but I still sensed some distrust in the animal's gaze.

The room was a disaster. Items lay about the floor as if a violent struggle had occurred. There wasn't any blood so I felt assured that she was still ok. I could see the beast was the only thing in the bedroom so I quickly shut the door and tied the rope again.

That's when it started to howl. The sound chilled my blood, which was already running cold because I still couldn't locate my daughter.

I continued through the house searching and analyzing our defenses. That's when I heard something large hit the outside of the house. I brought the gun up to the ready position and peeked out the front window. There I saw 2 more large wolves pacing in the front yard.

I caught the attention of one and it charged the house hitting the front door with all its might. I thought for sure the door was going to explode off its hinges. Luckily it didn't. It took every ounce of self-control not to pump a couple of the 1 oz. slugs I had in the shotgun into the beast.

My wife called down to me, assuring herself that I was ok. I told her I was and went up to make sure they were safe in that room. I recapped defensive shooting training they had received this past year, and then instructed them to relock the door.

I returned downstairs and took up a post sitting on the bottom steps to wait out the night. I could hear gunshots ringing out around the neighborhood but couldn't tell exactly where, just that they were close.

I woke up to the sound of the beast in my daughter's room scratching at the door. It was 4am now. I had hoped the night would pass so this nightmare would end. I did a quick calculation as to when the sun should start rising and figured I still had an hour and a half to go before I could see better outside to analyze the situation.

The wolf inside started howling like it was crying for help. That's when the two wolves outside started attacking the front door again. This time the door couldn't hold up to two large dogs hitting it, and it gave way.

The first wolf through the door caught one of my shotgun slugs to the right side of the body, dropping it immediately. I quickly racked another round and fired at the second as it lunged at me. I was falling backwards as it came at me, causing my shot to just miss center mass. The slug caught enough of the beast to drive it away though. It disappeared into the night, leaving a trail of blood behind.

The wolf that had collapsed upon the floor gasped for air as it slowly bled out. As the breaths became further and further apart, I noticed the fur on the beast start to change. Eventually it disappeared and was replaced with skin. The wolf changed into a teenage boy, now lying dead on my entry room floor.

In the confusion I didn't hear my wife and daughter yelling down to see if I was ok. They were now standing next to me looking at the dead boy on the floor.

"What did you do?" they asked. "You killed a boy!"

"He wasn't a boy when I shot him, I swear." I replied defensively.

"Why is he a boy now then?"

I didn't have an answer for that. I refused to believe that werewolves were real. I had lived my life knowing they were some fantasy-based monster.

I followed the trail of blood outside to look for the other wolf I had shot. It led down the street and out beyond anywhere I felt safe walking at that moment.

The sun was starting to light the east sky behind the mountains. I decided to wait until daylight had broken to continue my search for my daughter, then this second animal that I had wounded.

Upon entering the house, I took my family in my arms and held them tight. My wife and daughter were both crying. They were more worried about what was going to happen to me for shooting a person than what else had happened during the night. Then we heard a voice cry out.

"Daddy! I can't get out."

The words caught me by surprise. My youngest was calling to me from her bedroom. That's when I put one and one together and figured out that something in the world had changed overnight.

We ran to the bedroom door and quickly undid the rope allowing her to open the door and come out. We all pulled her to us holding her tight out of relief that she was ok.

"What happened to you?" I asked.

"I'm not sure," she said. "The last thing I remember is lying down to go to bed and then my whole body started hurting like my skin was bursting. Next thing I know I'm lying on my bed naked. I threw some jammies on and couldn't get out of my room."

I could hear police sirens in the distance. I turned to my family and told them to let me do the talking.

A single police car drove by the house. The officer was talking over his loudspeaker telling everyone to stay inside until further notice.

We propped the front door up in the jamb and I nailed it in place. We turned the radio on and learned that the world, much like our lives had definitely changed that night.

AN OPEN LETTER FROM MAXWELL DENTON

By Johnny Craft

To Anyone Who Finds This Letter,

My name is Maxwell Denton. I am a twenty-two-year-old pacifist from Milton, Massachusetts. I have very strong beliefs in compassion, equality, and love. In four days, I'm probably going to hurt a lot of people.

On June 22nd, our fine country turned savage. According to the news, a suspected 25% of us turned into werewolves that night. It only happened in America, and I don't think anyone knows why it happened. All we do know is, under a full moon, a lot of us turned into mindless, uncontrollable, murder puppets with no recollection of the horrors we created and the ripple effect it had on the lives and communities of the entire world.

Truth, Justice, and the American Way is literally a thing of the past. We have gone back to the days of suspicion and looking at your neighbor like they are the enemy. It is the Salem witch hunts all over again. It's McCarthy's Red Scare in the modern age. People look at each other like they are guilty of unspeakable evils, including me. I can't help but look at everyone I interact with and think, on the night of the 20th, they could have eaten one of my neighbors and even worse, in 4 days, they might do it again.

It's depressing these days. I feel alone all the time, even with the community surrounding me. I've seen lifelong friends turn on one another and resort to violence, all because they suspect the other to be a secret werewolf. No one remembers much of what happened that night, so how can anyone be accountable for their actions? How can you admit to an act that you're only somewhat sure you did?

How can you take responsibility for a transformation you had no control over? We all know that some of us HAD to have changed, but no one is willing to admit it or talk about what happened that night under the moon.

I understand why no one is willing to admit that they suspect they transformed into a surrogate savage for the evening. Our small town of Milton is riddled with paranoia. Telephone poles and shop windows used to display the occasional "Lost Pet" flyers, but those have been replaced with "Lost Person" posters. Within the last month, we've had more local funerals for people that I knew than I've ever experienced in my life. I watched a very good friend of mine beaten to death by three other guys because they thought he was responsible for killing Tina Dell. All I could do was pass by with my head down. It's better not to get involved with any of these conflicts. The last thing I want is for people to suspect me of being a wolf in human's clothing.

Tina Dell was the prettiest girl in my high school graduating class. Her death was the biggest shock to our community, probably because she was young and beautiful. That's usually how it works, right? I never knew much about her. I knew she played volleyball in school, loved baking and selling things at the local farmer's market, and I know that I ripped her throat out the night that everything changed.

When I woke up the morning of the 21st, the sun was just beginning to pierce the shadow of the night. I was lying naked in a field with Tina Dell next to me. Her body was bloodied, slashed and scraped and her throat was ripped open. Covered in my former classmate's blood, I rushed home in the hazy rays of the morning light and cleaned myself up before even trying to make sense of what happened.

I cried in the shower and decided that I needed to turn myself into the police. I thought I did something horrific during a sleepwalking episode. Doctors say I have a dopamine deficiency which can cause me to try to act out my dreams in my sleep on rare occasions. I thought that was a valid explanation for what had happened with me and Tina. I called Nine-One-One several times, but no one ever answered. That's when I turned on the news.

Werewolves! We somehow turned into werewolves! The transition from man to beast explained my sore throat and aching joints. I recall no details, no memories, of the transition itself. It was like blacking out from drinking or having a sudden seizure. The confusion of waking up after the transition was very similar to the times I've suffered from a sleepwalking episode.

Ironically, my life was dedicated to peace and humanity before all this happened. I had planned on joining the Peace Corps when I finished college. I wanted to help save lives, only to fall victim to a mysterious, involuntary brutality. How is that fair? Why was I chosen? I used to think I was genuinely a good person. I used to think that, deep down, human beings were good by nature. Now, after that night of horrific carnage, the biggest question on everyone's mind is, "Will it happen again, during the next full moon?" and I don't have an answer. I do know that something inside me feels different, since I changed. Maybe it was the human flesh I consumed when I was a wolf, but I went from being a vegetarian to having unnatural cravings for red meat. I feel like I am producing more testosterone. I'm working out more and having strange lusts for sex and violence that never existed inside of me before.

I've been keeping my head down and my mouth shut this past month. I'm shaving more often, to eliminate stubble and look less beastly, and spending my time alone, isolated from anyone else that I may harm during the next full moon. This note is to serve as my admission of my transition. I know I am a werewolf and I know that I changed on the night of June 22nd. I do not remember my actions, but I know in my heart that I am guilty.

I can honestly say that my life has changed. It's hard to find enjoyment, now. In the past, goals were always important to me and

I kept a calendar of all the things I wanted to do in a given week. Now, the only thing there is to look forward to is the next time the moon fills up, and what will happen. What will I be responsible for next time I change into a vicious animal, hell-bent on ripping apart human flesh?

I refuse to not take responsibility for myself. My basement door has been reinforced and I have stocked my downstairs fridge with plenty of red meat. After tomorrow night, I will lock myself in my home, hopefully ensuring the safety of the innocent people around me. I hope my plan works. If not, I fear that I will be responsible for a lot more deaths.

If someone finds this note before I transition back into a human, I beg you, please… PLEASE, do not kill me. I want to be a good person, despite the fact that I am a subconscious savage, I want to save lives and I want to atone for the wrongs I have done. I am responsible for those actions.

I am a pacifist who is a murderer. I am a gentle soul who is a violent beast. In the event of my death, I am not sure if anyone who knows me should mourn me. I am not sure if I deserve it.

Please Forgive Me,

Maxwell Denton

LONE RANGER
By Casey Little

"Get off me." I said as I narrowed my eyes at Mack who had his arm draped across my shoulders. He smiled down at me, but I was not amused.

"Come on Charlie, don't be such a stiff. This is a pool party, and you're out here in a t-shirt and long shorts. I can see that you are wearing a swim suit under it, so strip and jump in."

Jacob choked on his spit as he turned a bit red. "Mack! Have some decency. You don't just tell a girl to "strip" in public."

Mack waved his free hand at Jacob. "Ohhh please. We've known her for over four years, so I doubt she would take offense to my special charm. Besides, if I asked her to strip in the way you think I meant, I'm sure she'd be delighted to do it."

I shoved his arm off my shoulder and stood up.

"Over my dead body," I murmured.

Mack arched an eyebrow. "Ohh? Is that a challenge?" Mack said jokingly.

Jacob began to argue with Mack as I walked away. When Mack grabbed Jacob by the back of his shirt and the back of his swim shorts and flung him into the pool after yelling, "Hold your breath!" I stifled a laugh and kept walking.

I noticed Bree and Jess in their petite bikinis trying to impress the guys. I considered them vampires of the modern world. They lured in men, masked their constant interaction with the word "Relationship", and then, instead of bleeding their veins, sucked their wallets dry. Professional miners are what I liked to call them. That or "Thing One" and "Thing Two". Those names worked just as well.

I looked up at the trees above us and closed my eyes. I could feel the warmth of the sun, but then it all went cold as I was pulled into the present.

"Charlie!" A voice yelled. "Charlie, wake up."

I was ripped from the memory and pulled back into reality. Mack shook me awake. It was dark outside, and I could hear the rain on the roof of Cabin #4. I rose from my cot and stared at the two men. "What do you want?"

"Jess is dead; Bree killed her after turning into some kind of animal." Jacob said. His complexion was sickly pale and the rain had plastered his hair to his head. He was out of breath and clearly had been in a full out sprint from the main cabin up the hill.

I blinked rapidly trying to comprehend the new information. "What?"

Jacob's story seemed like the plot to an unbelievable Sci-fi movie, but then he pulled up the clip on his phone. The reporter's expression was devoid of emotion. The camera shook unsteadily in an effort to focus on the reporter sitting at the desk. There was a loud banging noise from somewhere within the news room. The reporter stammered and spoke quickly.

"This is breaking news. All across the US there have been spontaneous outbreaks of some unknown disease that has caused thousands or perhaps millions to mutate into what we believe to be werewolves. Here is live footage that was captured from one of our news vans. This may be disturbing to some viewers."

The screen changed to a view from within a van. By the light of the streetlamps it was possible to see that there were massive furry shapes quickly vanishing in and out of the shadows. The camera panned to see a man running down the street towards the van. The news staff yelled for him to hurry as one of the furred creatures began to pursue him. The creature chased and pounced, stopping the man abruptly. There was a blur of fangs and blood, and then there was an unsettling growl that emanated from the beast.

The wolf creature then lifted its now blood covered maw, turning towards the camera. The thing had the fur and head of a wolf with the body structure of a large human. Werewolves had just become a reality, and the world now knew the human race had a natural predator.

"You're kidding me. This is for real?" Mack said. Looking at Jacob, "This is a joke, right?"

Irritation crept into Jacob's expression. "Do I look like someone who just sprinted for my life, from the Main Cabin all the way to Cabin #4, just for fun while it's raining?"

"You got a point." I said. "Pack your stuff and let's go. We need to get to the Main Cabin."

Jacob whirled on me, "And go out there to be food for those things?! I don't think so! You'd have to be crazy!"

"Then so be it." I said. "Going to town is not an option. The main cabin has the provisions that we will need to ride this thing out for however long this takes. The sooner we get there the better."

Mack nodded in agreement and began to pack his things in his bag. I did the same. Jacob just stood there.

"I'm not going back; that thing is still out there!" Jacob said raising his voice.

I turned to him and slammed his back against the wall. "You need to chill. That thing will still be out there whether we are in here or up there. It will continue to be there until it is killed. I'm sure suicide is not programmed into its brain and there aren't any hunters in the area because this is a protected National Park."
Mack and Jacob stared at me.

"I don't care what you decide to do. Stay if you want. I'm going up there with or without you." I said and released Jacob. I returned to my cot and finished putting in the last of my things in my backpack, shouldered it, and opened a wooden box that was sitting next to my bag.

Lifting the lid revealed the silver-plated metal of a six-shot revolver along with three boxes of .45 caliber bullets. I shoved two of the boxes into my pocket and opened the third, loading six into the gun. Closing the box, I shoved it into the pocket with the others.

I paced over to the door and slid the revolver into the leather holster. Wrapping the gun belt around my waist I tightened and secured it. Looking back Jacob had perched on the end of my cot and Mack held a double barrel shotgun wearing his bag on his back.

"Okay, let's go." I said to Mack.

Jacob's head snapped up and his eyes widened. "You're really going to leave me here by myself?"

"Yeah, last time I checked you were old enough to make your own decisions. You get to choose how you will live or how you will die. I am focused on myself right now. I'm not living anymore, I'm surviving. You should probably learn the difference."

I unlocked the door to Cabin #4 and turned back to Jacob. "If you change your mind, you know where we'll be. Lock the door when we leave." I then threw him Cabin #4's key ring and picked up the main cabin's keys off the desk.
I opened the door and Mack and I ran out into the dark.

Fifteen minutes down the trail at a jogging pace Mack finally spoke up.

"Don't you think that was a bit harsh? You know how Jacob is."

"No, not really. Why?" I said.

"I don't know if you knew but he really likes you."

"I know."

Mack looked at me surprised. "What? You knew?" he said.

"I'm not blind Mack. If I can track birds in the snow, I think I can pick up on the mate selection advances of a human male towards a female."

Mack laughed quietly. "That is a weird way to put it, but you've got a point." He said.

I heard the rustle before I heard the growl. A massive black furred beast leapt from behind some bushes to the left. I reached out within that split second and shoved Mack out of the way to the ground.

"It found us, get up." I snarled.

Mack scrambled to his feet and I pulled the revolver from its holster. The beast spun in that moment to face us once again and launched itself into the air. It had the reflexes of an advanced predator. I pulled Mack out of the way again kneeling down just out of range of the beast's claws.

I aimed at the last second and fired as the beast landed. Its jaws were open, lined with white fangs that were aimed for my throat.

The slug entered the beast's mouth and exited out of the back of its neck. The beast didn't slow due to its tremendous momentum traveling forward but instead its head dropped and connected with the ground sending it into a somersault.

Even with my effort of diving to the side a claw still grazed my shoulder in the confusion of the beast's tumble. Mack got back to his feet uttering curses as I ran after the beast that finally sprawled onto the ground on its back.

Without a thought crossing my mind, I lined the revolver's barrel up with the beast's head and squeezed the trigger once and then twice. Then again, and again, and again, until there was nothing left to fire. Still, I squeezed the trigger over and over despite the empty click of the gun's hammer.

In the time that it took Mack to reach me, I saw the beast transform into a human form, that looked strangely like Bree. She had been shot repeatedly in the head just as I had shot the beast.

What did I just do? I still squeezed the trigger over and over. Click. Click. Click. Then it stopped. I looked down at the gun to see a hand on it. It then gently pulled the gun from my grasp and I let it go. Mack then appeared into view.

Oh…I had forgotten about him.

"Charlie." he said. "Charlie, are you okay?"

"Yeah," I said bewildered, "I think so."

Mack turned me away from the body.

"Did I get it?" I asked.

"Yeah, you got it."

When I went to turn around Mack stopped me. "Don't worry about it right now. Let's just get to the main cabin for now. I'll bury it tomorrow. Okay?" He spoke. I nodded slowly and walked away letting myself be steered by Mack. I felt lightheaded and like I was going to be sick, but I just kept walking.

We arrived at the main cabin and Mack opened the heavy wooden door. Then I passed out. I woke up lying on my stomach with a bucket lying beside me, a bowl with water in it with a wash rag draped over the side. There was a slight sour smell in the room. I realized it was the smell of puke and my stomach heaved. Nope….nope…nope. Not doing it.

I sat up and swung my feet over the side of the cot. My head felt like it was ready to split and my stomach knotted. Food was the last thing I wanted to think about but I was starving. I opened my door and was blinded by sunlight that poured in the windows. I then heard the shouts coming from the lobby.

As I walked down the hall the voices got louder.

"How could you let that happen!? When you went with her, I thought you would save her life NOT the other way around!" I heard a familiar voice yell.

Jacob? He made it. I felt my shoulders relax just a bit.

"So what? We are alive and that is what matters. With that thing dead, there are still plenty of things out there that would be more than happy to eat us. Just thought I'd let you know in case you've forgotten that." Mack's voice was barely above his normal talking voice.

His voice was naturally loud so it didn't take much for him to match Jacob's hysteric squalling.

I stepped into the lobby and Jacob's eyes widened. "Charlie." He came over and hugged me. A sharp pain seared in my shoulder, I grunted in pain and shoved him away. I probably shoved him harder than I had meant to because the look he gave me was quite odd.

I reached up grabbing my shoulder. "Sorry, my shoulder. I hurt it last night and I need to..." I trailed off as I felt the bandages beneath my shirt.

My eyes shot straight to Mack.

His expression softened and I would have laughed at his black eye except there were more important things to attend to.

I narrowed my eyes and said, "Mack I need to talk to you."

He shook his head and gestured to his eye with a smile. "Oh this? Nah, don't worry about it. I never knew that you were such a fighter while you're unconscious. God, you hit hard when you're serious. It took me a little bit to get you to calm down. Then you started puking your guts out."

Mack shrugged. "Surprised the heck out of me; now I know why you're so mean in the morning. You got a sharp elbow too...

took one of those to the ribs." Mack said as he rubbed his side gingerly.

"Mack." I started again but was cut off by Mack who narrowed his eyes and looked at Jacob. When Jacob turned around Mack's expression changed instantly to a smile.

"I'm sure you're both hungry; I've fixed breakfast so let's eat." Mack said.

The meal was a quiet one and we both ignored Jacob's skeptical looks that repeatedly went from Mack to me and then back again. He knew something was up.

After we ate, I went outside to look for the beast. My memory from last night was fuzzy. It had happened all too fast. It had been a miracle in itself that I had killed the thing. I remember firing the gun and the beast charging at me, but that was it. Anything before or after, I had no idea, but I was sure that Mack remembered everything.

I needed to pull him aside and talk to him.

Just then I heard something from behind me. I was grabbed and then suddenly slammed against the side of the cabin. I grimaced because of my shoulder and when I opened my eyes I came face to face with Mack.
He had never been that rough before but then too he was always the one getting hit; never the other way around.

His face was inches from mine and I was suddenly grateful for his annoying habit of eating peppermints all the time. His eyes peered into mine; they carried a strict and serious gaze.

"What happened?" he said.

"What do you mean?"

"You know what I mean."

"I don't." I started, but he cut me off.

"Don't play stupid. I saw the scars on your back. What the hell happened?"

"That happened in the past, leave it alone."

"No" he pressed me harder against the cabin's wall.

"Tell me." he demanded.

"Why do you want to know? Why are you suddenly interested in my business all of a sudden? What does my past have to do with you?" I snapped back.

"Everything." he said simply.

"What does…?" He cut me off again.

"What happened in your past that made you able to move like that? Huh? Because what you did last night was not normal. I didn't have time to react to the first attack so how did you manage to move like that?"

"What do you mean?" I asked.

Mack heaved a sigh and let me go. He walked a few paces away and then came back. He jammed his hands into his pockets.

"What I want to know is what happened in your past that gave you those scars. Whatever it was gave you the ability to save my life twice, kill a werewolf with a six-shot revolver and escape with a scratch on the shoulder before I could so much as understand that we were being attacked." he said finally.

"I just want to know." he said after a brief silence.

I took a deep breath.

"A bear. I was attacked by a bear okay. I was 7 years old and nobody helped me. I'm a park ranger now so I can make sure that there will at least be one park ranger that is willing to help a terrified child that is being mauled and eaten alive. That there will be at least one ranger that will not run away, like they ran away from me and left me to die."

Mack just stared in disbelief.

I sighed and let myself slide against the side of the cabin to the ground. I sat there.

"Did that answer your question? Since you just had to know, I hope you feel better knowing." I said.

There was a familiar click of a gun's hammer being pulled back. We both looked over to see Jacob holding the silver revolver from the night before. His eyes looked sunken into his skull, he was pale and he looked sick. I was sure that neither of us liked the look in his eyes.

"Well that is a really touching story. Now that you've gotten all personal and buddy buddy, I'd like to know why I've been left out. Why are you keeping secrets? Huh? I'd just like to know as to why I've been out of the loop for four years." Jacob said.

His head twitched slightly and his eyes were bloodshot.

"Jacob, you need to take your medication." I said calmly.

Jacob looked at me and laughed. "They're gone. All gone." His laugh grew hysterical. "I lost them when I ran out to you last night. I've been out of that loop too. Oh. That makes two loops now. Well aren't I just out of it?"

"You're not in your right mind either Jacob." Mack said. "Now please put down the gun before someone gets hurt.

Jacob stared at me and then at Mack. He looked back at me and said, "You know what? You're right Mack. I'm not in my right mind."

Jacob pointed the revolver at Mack and pulled the trigger.

"No!" I screamed.

USING THE SCIENTIFIC METHOD

By Marie Newbold

Step I: Hypothesis
June 28, 2024 – Half-Moon, waning

Dr. Lisa Holcomb cleared her throat as she shuffled her papers on the table. It was one of the steel lab tables on the third floor, not the comfortable guest conference table on the first floor. A week ago, the wooden table had been smashed to bits when the five-foot tall department secretary had become a wolf between pouring punch and passing out cookies. Not to be outdone by the staff, two of the eight professors and six of the twenty graduate students had also grown fangs and claws. If not for going home due to a family emergency, Lisa would most likely have become part of the bloodied bits found dangling from the jaws of the wolf when the vet students started tranquilizing all furry moving things they came in contact with.

The surviving members of Southern Illinois University's medicine and biochemistry departments gathered around Lisa. At only thirty-eight years old, Lisa was the senior most faculty member left even though she had only three years full time teaching experience. Sturdy farmhands were intermixed with Asian immigrants in an unlikely mix of ethnicities for a small Southern Illinois town. All eyes were shadowed with loss and fear. No one looked up to meet Lisa's eyes; no one even acknowledged her noisy paper shuffle. Lisa sympathized; thirty percent of the country had died on a single night when a quarter of their peers had become big, bad wolves that had a taste for man. The death rates exceeded the death tolls experienced during the entire ten-year run of the Black Death. America had three weeks until the next full moon to figure out what happened and how to stop it from happening again. The CDC had just added Lisa to the roster of researchers to discover what had happened and how to stop it, but first she had to bring these kids around. She couldn't sift through all the data on her own. She rubbed her forehead with her left hand and decided to try tough love.

She brought her hand down from her forehead onto the table like a judge's gavel. Her hand made a ringing noise against the steel dissection table which made all seven students jump with surprise. "Here's what's going on kids," Lisa said, putting all her resolve into her voice. "The CDC has just agreed that I'm qualified to examine all the medical records to figure out who is going to be a werewolf next full moon and who is not. Since the vet boys successfully proved that sedating works on the wolves without damaging the human, we can stave off another disaster during the next full moon. So let's go over what we need to do next." Lisa met seven pairs of eyes. Five held hope that they might survive next time. Two held fear of what they would do next time the moon was full.

"First off, let's talk about possible triggers. We know that 25% of the total population became a full wolf. What does that suggest to us?"

"A recessive gene, like blue eyes or the PTC bitter taste receptor." Rubaina Gupta was an amazing researcher from Aurangabad, India. According to Rubaina, her home was a smaller city of only 1.3 million. She had also become a wolf a week ago. Her boyfriend Lee Williams had managed to lock her in a janitor's closet comprised of concrete walls and a steel door until she had become human again. He still limped from the wolf's attempts to hamstring him.

Lisa smiled at Rubaina. "Exactly. We all know that large chunks of the genetic code tell the body whether or not to produce specific enzymes. This is the source of the AB blood typing system, after all. So we need to take the data from the CDC and compare our patients. If we can find that all the people who turned into werewolves also have blood type A positive, then we can figure out why having that

140

particular protein hanging on your blood cells makes a patient hungry for human meat once a month or so and, most importantly, STOP IT." With another drop of her hand, Lisa brought her students back to life. "This is our profession, ladies and gentleman. Our profession has figured out how to fix everything from pancreas failures to a lack of neurotransmitters in the brain. We should be thinking of the werewolves as patients. It is unfortunate that their condition poses extreme danger to anyone in their vicinity, but at no time should we give up, sit on our hands, and cry. We can beat this."

As Lisa scanned the faces of her students again, she found less shadows, and more shock. Eyes held glimmers of hope. She put her hands in her lap to hide their tremor and let her words sink in. As the shock wore off and hope crept in, she continued the meeting. "Now, Mahinder, let's catch up on that blood work that I asked you to do. Would you like to present your findings?" The students, desperate for any nugget of hope, turned to their science to solve the problem.

Lisa turned on her smart phone to record Mahinder's presentation. Her home screen held a picture of two teenage boys who smiled out at her, trusting her to find an answer. The tears blurred the picture on the phone, making it difficult to enter her unlock code. Fellow genetic researchers had taken years to find partial solutions to severe depression after identifying the chemical and genetic factors that caused it. The search for a solution to lycanthropy had just begun. The chances of having a cure in the next three weeks were faint, at best.

Step II: Research
July 4, 2024 – New Moon

Etta Holcomb made a last tour of her tiny cabin. She patted her wedding photo, and Davy's high school graduation photo. She straightened the painting that she had made last year, an impressionist rendition of a photo she had taken in the Serengeti. She had already taken care of the more mundane things, liking clearing out the refrigerator and removing the flowers from the vases. She hummed as she patted her favorite things, visualizing a net of serenity over the cabin. When she felt the moment was right, she clapped her hands and turned her back on her home. A large green backpack sat by the door, more appropriate to a college student than a Grandma, but Etta preferred it anyway.

Etta had always listened to her intuition. When she met George for the first time, she knew that he would become her friend for life. When George had passed on after forty years of marriage, she knew that she had to find a new life for herself and had taken off to see the world over the objections of all three of her children. Yesterday, when her grandson Cory had confessed that he was afraid of himself and that he didn't think his mom would find a cure, Etta had felt that familiar stirring in her gut that meant she had to do something.

Etta picked the backpack up as she walked out the front door, carefully closing and locking the door behind her. She believed that her energy would protect the cottage, but a good lock never hurt either. Stowing the backpack in the passenger seat of the Jeep, she walked down the lane to Hank and Daisy's tiny house. Last night, Etta had recruited the younger woodworkers to look after her cabin while she was gone. Today, she left the key with a worn and worried Daisy before returning to her Jeep and the road.

It took Etta an hour and a half to make it out of Missouri. The drive was much easier listening to the witty conversation of Bill Kurtis and Paula Poundstone. The show currently on the radio was a pre-recorded one, since Bill Kurtis had died and Paula Poundstone was missing. As KRCU moved on from the comedy quiz show, Cape Girardeau suburbs appeared on either side of the highway.

"This is KRCU, Cape Girardeau, your National Public Radio Station... It's eighty-seven degrees today along the banks of the Mississippi River, and rain is expected next Tuesday. In the meantime, remember that today we're celebrating July 4th with our National Guard. The troops will be mixing it up with local folk band A Perfect Fifth at Riverside Park from 5 PM to 8 PM, followed by

fireworks at 9 PM.

"Stay tuned for All Things Considered, where ACLU President Aiken Wilco will be discussing the upcoming Lycanthrope Identification Bill that is shooting through the Federal House and Senate like a rocket, scorching everyone in its path. But first, a word from our sponsors..." As a local hospital discussed their outpatient care center, Etta approached the wide open space around the I-146 Bridge into Illinois. Just over the bridge, across the levee, and then a left and up the road for an hour, and Etta would be on the highway which would take her straight to her grandsons.

The Illinois side of the bridge was blocked with military men. Men and women were deprived of their identity due to face shields, riot gear, and helmets that obscured their faces and covered their bodies so the only way to tell them apart was their height. They looked vaguely like dark pins in a bowling alley. They were faced towards the Illinois state line, except for four soldiers facing a nearby pickup. The pickup was shiny, copper colored, and swarming with young men holding hunting rifles. The young men were watching the state line while they chatted. The dark soldiers were quiet, focused on the bridge.

Etta parked her Jeep at the bridge and waited while an investment group on the radio explained why it was better than other groups. When their explanations were over, and the croaky voiced reporter began to interview the new head of the ACLU, Etta turned down the radio and gently honked her horn. The soldiers jumped, but the young men in the pickup truck tumbled and two of their guns went off. The four soldiers facing them marched over to disarm the "support group". Thankfully, the guns had been pointed low. The only casualty was the tire on the shiny pickup.

Etta's Jeep, cheerfully painted yellow with green and blue flower petals, did not earn the grandmother much in the way of respect from the soldiers. A figure of middling height and above average breadth approached the car. "Ma'am, what are you doing here?" The voice and shoulders revealed the male gender, and the name "Vellini" was stitched in yellow on his chest.

"Trying to cross the bridge."

"Why? This is the safe side. We've seen fires and heard all kinds of noises from over there."

Etta bit her lower lip, refrained from making chicken-crossing-the-road references by applying a healthy dose of self-preservation in the face of the large gun the man held, and replied, "My grand-children need me, so I'm going to Illinois. Can you let me pass, please?"

The man behind the shaded riot gear helmet may have looked surprised, saddened, worried, or been sticking his tongue out at Etta. Given how long it took for him to respond, he could have done any number of things. After being something-ed from behind the mirrored mask for quite long enough, Etta put the Jeep in park, left it idling, and took a drink of water from her cup on the dash. She returned her cup to the holder, and then looked back at Vellini. "Well? Will you move?" she asked.

"Ma'am, I don't know if you've heard the news from across the river, but..."

"But a bunch of people looked like wolves a little while ago and a bunch of other people died. Yes son, I do have a radio. But, as I said, my grandchildren need me. I don't care if I catch the bubonic plague or a nuclear missile up my backside; I will go to those kids. Now can you ask those five gentlemen to shuffle ten feet to the left for two minutes? I really do need to be on my way." Her bob of silver hair and liver spots aside, Vellini was no match for stubborn Etta, and he knew it. Three minutes later, the Jeep was on the bridge and Etta was waving goodbye to black riot gear and Missouri, the land of the humans. As she passed burned-out cars with scorch marks down the side, she wondered what land she was entering.

Step III: Experiment
July 13, 2024 — Half-Moon, Waxing

Davy winced as the coffee scalded his tongue. If Lisa had been there instead of rushing off to the lab at the crack of dawn, she would have been teasing him for drinking the coffee before it cooled. Davy couldn't shake the feeling that her research into a "scientific" answer was only a way to avoid the problem at home. How on earth would one-quarter of the people only on American soil be afflicted, if this werewolf thing were an illness like Lisa claimed? Clenching his jaw in frustration, Davy refused to think about their recent arguments. He was going to get something concrete and useful done before the next full moon.

Taking another sip of the scalding black coffee Davy joined his older son on the couch. The patches on the sofa were still holding up, the floral print giving the living room a more country feel than it had previously. Last month, Davy would have propped his foot on the coffee table. Today, Davy's right foot rose up of its own volition, dropping to the floor with a thud when it failed to encounter its normal resting place. Cory, almost as tall as his father now that he was on the cusp of adulthood, looked at his father's foot with a scowl before returning his attention to CNN.

"The CDC is being sued by the ACLU for releasing unnecessary medical information on patients without proper consent forms. The civil rights group is defending those individuals who changed into wolf form, stating that just because a person was afflicted with the transition is no reason to prosecute their daily lives between full moons.

"The CDC has released a statement that they are acting in accordance with all federal laws relating to patient privacy. Meanwhile, Senator Guitterez of Texas is rallying support for his "Lycanthrope Identification and Suppression Bill", citing protection of non-shifting humans during the next full moon as his primary goal."

Davy managed to find the remote and flipped the channel to Dr.

Oz. Oddly enough, Dr. Oz still managed to make a living helping people identify proper weight loss methods. Cory's eyes almost became visible to Davy, before dropping to his father's work boot next to the blue foot brace that Cory was wearing. He shifted his glass of water from left to right and back again while scratching his shoulder blades against the back of the couch.

Davy cleared his throat twice and then nudged Cory with his elbow. "Where's Will?"

Cory's eyebrows came together. "He left on his bike a half-hour ago. He didn't say where he was going."

Davy nodded, filling in the scene from memories of previous weeks. Cory trying to talk to his younger brother Will; Will ignoring any words coming out of his older brother's mouth. Will leaving the house as early as possible; Cory's hunched shoulders and hidden tears. Davy had followed Will a week ago to make sure that he wasn't doing something dangerous. He'd found his younger son digging a large pit, and loose sticks to the side. It looked like Will was prepping a trap in case he was chased by a certain brotherly wolf again. Davy had left material out that would improve the trap without saying anything to Will. Will had taken the material immediately. Davy wished his younger son luck.

"How's the foot? Are you walking without crutches yet?" Davy nodded down to the blue boot as he asked this question.

"Yeah. I can't flex or twist the ankle yet, but I can hobble okay. Mom says I should be good to remove the boot next week." Both of them tensed. Three weeks ago and a week in the future were difficult times to talk about. "What's the backup plan if I'm moving well, Dad?" Cory whispered softly.

A horn wheezed from the driveway. Davy and Cory looked up from the boot to see a truck with a green door, a blue hood, and a body with more repaired rusty spots than original body in the driveway. Cory looked at Davy with surprise on his face. "What's Mr.

Sommers doing here, Dad?"

Davy stared out the window, not looking at his son. "Hal is the best welder I've ever met. Your mother is looking for the long solution, and I hope that she finds it. In the meantime, we all have to survive the next full moon. Hal is here to help me make cages. I've also saved all the tranquilizer darts that I can." Davy looked back at Cory, whose jaw had dropped open. "We'll bar the outer windows against others who might be wolves and gunnin' for us. You'll be safe in the basement. The tranqs will be there if the bars don't hold. IF there is a next time, which I really wish everyone would realize is not a certain thing." Davy clapped his hands on Cory's shoulders. "I won't let you be hurt again, but I won't let you hurt anyone else, either. I love you all too much." Davy paused, giving Cory time to protest being caged. His son didn't though, just shook his head, and then nodded at his dad before hobbling back to his bedroom.

Davy went out to meet Hal, a little gnome of a man with a grimy hat and patched overalls. Hal was pulling cage panels out of the back of his pick-up. "Hey there, Davy. These are the kinds of cages that the Forest Service uses for bears and lions and the like. I figure we can use the panels to wall off where you'n want. We can bolt the panels to the floor if you've a concrete basement floor, or we can weld the panels together if you'n don't. Which do you'n have?"

Davy nodded. "Concrete floors. Let's do this."

Hal pulled a large tool case from the cab and returned to the back of the truck. "This was smart. There's a few other folks that are putting in cages and such, but you'n's the only one I know who's putting in a double line of defense. All them cows, makes sense. I bet the wolves ran for them cows lickety-split. How many cows did you lose last time?"

"A few." It was true that Davy had lost some of his dairy herd on the night of the last full moon, since Cory wasn't the only wolf that Davy had subdued that night. Davy wasn't about to discuss with Hal, or any other man, what it had felt like to have his teenage son turn into a wolf mid-video game and try to eat his younger son. "Let's get this done as soon as possible. Lisa thinks she can cure all the wolves, so I need to get these installed as a done deal before she gets home."

Hal winked. "Ah, the missus must be protected, whether she will or no. I gotcha, I gotcha. Off to work we go." Whistling all the way, Hal carried his load off to begin making cages.

Step IV: Data
July 21, 2024 – Full Moon at 6:57 PM

Will was helping Grandma E cook dinner when Mom crashed through the back door. Tonight, even Will noticed how tired Mom looked.

"How are they?" Grandma E asked Mom.

Mom's first response, while verbal, wasn't something that Will was supposed to say in front of his Grandma. "Considering that they are all convinced that they are going to die, but they can't let me help them thanks to the good Senator of Kick-all-Lycanthropes-while-they're-down, just dandy. They're having a little picnic from the loft, and the cages are ready."

"Why can't we join them, Mom?" Will had met Lee and Rubaina before. They seemed kind of cool, for adults.

"Because by the terms of the new law, if I see someone change into a werewolf tonight I have to report it. If I don't see it, I can't report it. They're protecting me so that I can keep working." With a huge sigh, Will's mom deflated. "But it's that same law that makes it so none of them can see Cory tonight, so I guess we all just have to suffer through." Mom gave Will a hug, and then reached around to grab the mashed potatoes. "Let's eat this dinner and get through tonight, huh champ?"

Mom was serving meatloaf.

Will wondered about the wisdom of serving a meat log on this particular night. Grandma E at his side or not, though, Will wasn't insane enough to question his mother's judgment. Not this time.

"I hope we can go into town for ice cream tomorrow," Cory said. "I really want some cookie dough ice cream. How 'bout you, Will? What are you going to get?" Cory's voice was casual, as if this wasn't a night that disaster was going to repeat itself, as if the rest of the family wasn't going to be an emotional wreck by morning. Will almost hated his brother then.

He turned to give Cory several reasons why he wouldn't be available for ice cream tomorrow, but made the mistake of looking into his brother's eyes. As had happened each of the three or four times since last month, Will could only see fangs snapping at him from underneath those same green eyes. His words died on his tongue, as he remembered his brother imitating Professor Lupin in the *Lego: Harry Potter* game – uncontrollable hunger for recent playmates included.

A sharp kick on the ankle from Grandma E startled Will back into the present. "Uh, the chocolate peanut butter sounds good," Will managed to stutter in the general direction of the image of Thor on Cory's t-shirt. The Norse god slumped down with its wearer, until only the hammer was visible. Will tried to find a way to apologize. He did understand that whatever had happened last month, Cory didn't remember it. But Will couldn't forget it, either.

It was a quiet meal. Mom looked exhausted, defeated, and a little ill. She picked at her food, concentrating on the vegetables, all the fight gone. Cory was still slumped across the table, not eating anything. Will picked at his food, nibbling the green beans and cornbread.

Grandma E never ate much anyway, but she had seemed really sad ever since she limped up the lane a week ago and grabbed Will and Cory into a huge hug. She wasn't driving her awesome flower child Jeep, and she reeked like Dad after he'd been fencing in a pasture. She wouldn't answer Dad's normal questions about her trip, just said it was "really long". She was nibbling even less than Will, but she seemed happier here than wherever she had been.

Only Will's dad continued to shove food into his mouth in a continuous, business-like manner. Will normally saw his dad eat like this when he was waiting for a heifer to birth a calf and Cory called it being in the Farmer Zone. When Dad's plate was cleared, he looked around the table, then at the clock. "It's now 6:00, folks. We've got less than an hour to get set. Everyone eat what you can, you've got to keep your strength up." Dad's gaze pulled Cory up straight. "Especially you, son. You may not remember last full moon, but surely you remember how weak you were the following morning. You'll need your strength tonight."

"Hey, Dad, I think I should remind you that in an hour, you all are going to hope I'm not strong enough to get out of that cage. I should be doing something to weaken myself." Cory tried to laugh off his upcoming canine state, but it came out as sort of a croak.

"I'll need to be in the cage, as well." Grandma E announced. "You won't know if I'm a wolf or not until the full moon, so I'll need to be locked away."

"Oh no you don't!" Cory jumped out of his chair, stomping back and forth on the far side of the table. "We KNOW that I will be a wolf. If you're not, I'll kill you and find you tomorrow morning. I WON'T do that. "

"Well, of course not, my boy." Grandma E turned to Mom. "You said that those vet students proved that tranquilizers worked, right?" At Mom's hesitant nod, Grandma nodded "Well, then we just have to dose ourselves sleepy, right, Cory? I know I'm supposed to be a good influence, and all, but there's always marijuana. Or we could steal that bottle of vodka your mom keeps for making strawberry ice cream and do shots until you can't stand. A drunken wolf can't be that dangerous."

Jaws dropped around the table, as the family of four looked at the sixty-year-old woman. "What?" she asked, watery eyes dancing with mirth. "You do know I married Grandpa George AFTER going to Woodstock with him, right? I could suggest all kinds of fun ways to make you unable to walk, but I think we'd better just stick with the light stuff." A thin hand waved at her son. "You can always shoot whichever of us gets furry with your tranq gun. You don't get any vodka."

Mom looked at Dad, and Dad looked at Mom. Their grins could have spooked people at Halloween. Mom rose to give Cory a huge hug. "Well, hon? Do you think you can stand this? I think it's actually a pretty good idea. After all, all the Civil War doctors carried spirits. You're too young to take the sleeping meds that the kids outside are using, but we can give you just enough alcohol to slow you down."

Cory had tears pouring down his cheeks. "I won't kill Grandma. Promise me I won't kill Grandma."

"You know I trust my gut in all things," Grandma said, "and I'm sure that you're not going to kill me tonight." Cory just shook his head in denial.

Will stared around at the adults who had spent the past ten years telling him about the evils of drinking and drug use. "Are you insane? This is your answer? Do that one thing that we should never, ever, do? And we're all supposed to laugh and be happy now?"

Dad gave Will a chuff on the shoulder. "Well, there's this little difference between not drinking when too much alcohol could screw up your life, and imbibing alcohol as a medicine in extreme circumstances. I say drink up, son."

Will watched his grandma grab a blanket for the cage and head downstairs. "When I turn fourteen, are you going to get me drunk on vodka and lock me in a cage?"

151

Cory snuffled back his tears. "Absolutely. Then you can puke and have a hangover the next morning too. Isn't that what happens to people who drink?" He grabbed two juice glasses and the vodka bottle that his mom held out from the kitchen, and then turned to the basement stairs. The house had been locked up before dinner, so all that was left was to keep vigil over Grandma and Cory.

Will smacked Cory on the shoulder while carefully avoiding looking at his eyes and raced downstairs ahead of his brother. The cage that Hal and Dad had built was the size of a large closet and contained some of the wicker furniture from the porch. Grandma was already inside, and patted the seat next to her for Cory. Cory sat as far away from Grandma E as he could and passed her a glass. They each drank a glass of vodka while Dad locked up the cage. Cory coughed and gagged, then forced down more. Grandma E patted Cory on the back, and then rested her hand on his shoulder. Cory shuddered, and drank some more vodka.

Dad handed Will a second tranq gun. "Okay, son. I don't know what the rules of this werewolf thing are. Just in case, you'll be my backup." Dad showed Will how to load, release the safety, and fire the pistol. Will had been shooting rifles at targets for two years now, and had taken down his first deer last fall. He gripped the pistol tightly, and went to stand near where Dad leaned against the worktable. Mom came over to put her arm around Will's shoulder, and her hand gripped Dad's hip pocket so tightly that her knuckles were white. She shuddered and buried her face in Dad's shirt. The clock said 6:53 pm.

THE RECRUIT
By Johnny Craft

I need savages.

The last full moon, we were attacked by werewolves! I ain't yankin' ya. Honest to goodness, actual werewolves, like something out of a frickin' horror movie.

I went on the offensive, when I put together what was happening. I'm an avid hunter, so why not be a monster hunter? I grabbed my favorite rifle, headed out to the woods, climbed up into a tree, and hoped to take one of these suckers by surprise.

It became pretty apparent, pretty quickly, that I wasn't going to be able to take out every one of them. There were too many of them here in Quincy, and since this was happening everywhere, it seemed like humanity was wicked screwed. Instead of picking off beasts one by one, from up in my perch, I just sat there frozen, sweating bullets, and hoping none of them spotted me.

I watched a werewolf chase a young girl through the woods. I put my scope up to my eye, to get a closer look at the carnage. I'm ashamed to admit that I had no intention of pulling the trigger on my rifle. No B.S., I was just gonna sit in a tree and watch this, probably teen, girl get torn to bits instead of giving away my position. I felt like the biggest coward on the east coast at that very moment.

That's when I got my renewed sense of inspiration.

Some skinny kid came running into the fray, shirtless, with not a defined muscle on his body. He was wielding a butcher knife that he probably got from his mother's kitchen. He was screaming bloody murder, trying to get that thing's attention. Unlike me, who fancies himself a real "man's man", sitting on a branch, cowering like a complete rube.

The werewolf sank its teeth deep into the girl's throat. No way she coulda survived something like that. The young guy wasted no time sticking that knife directly into the werewolf's eye, though, in an attempt to save her life. I haven't seen such bravery since the ninth round of the first Gatti-Ward fight.

It wasn't enough to kill that sci-fi abomination, but it was enough to inspire me to stop being such a baby. That furry bastard backhanded the kid right into a tree, knocking him unconscious. The werewolf hovered above the guy, ready to have a second helping of human throat.

BAM!

I took my shot, hitting ol' Wolfman in the upper shoulder. It didn't even look like it wounded the thing, if I'm being honest. But, it was enough to cause the creature to go running. It was enough to save at least one life. I don't know if the kid was incredibly ballsy, or incredibly stupid, but he earned some mercy.

I stayed awake all frickin' night, watching over him. I could see his chest rising up and down, so I knew the wolf didn't off the kid, but he didn't wake up until daylight broke. He noticed the dead girl next to him and ran off, horrified, before I got the chance to come down from the tree and talk to him. I was able to follow him and figure out where he lived, though.

Instead of knocking on his door, I decided to gather my thoughts and formulate a plan. I wanted to watch some news. See what the experts had to say. I ain't about to approach a kid after the most traumatic moment of his life. These things require time to process mentally.

In the coming days, I lowkey stalked him. Seemed like he lived in a small house by himself. Probably a college kid. I needed to approach him before the next full moon, though, when everyone thought people would change again. It was hard to know who you could feel safe around. Everyone walked around, looking at everyone else like they were secret werewolves. The only person I knew I could absolutely trust was this scrawny fella.

The morning before the next full moon, I packed up all my guns and ammo into two duffel bags. One for me, one for the recruit. I was still unsure how I was gonna pitch the idea to him, but it couldn't be that hard of a sell. Last time, he went after a monster with a kitchen knife. I doubt he would say no to a bag full of high-powered killing machines.

Standing outside of his house, I watched him close all of his curtains, so I knew he was home. No one answered the door when I knocked. I tried the doorknob, fully expecting it to be locked. It wasn't, so I let myself in.

The place was pretty trashed, lending a lot more plausibility to my buddy being a college student. Either that, or the events of the past month were so overwhelming that he didn't feel like cleaning up was a priority anymore. Before I got the chance to call out to him, I noticed a handwritten note on a table next to the door.

This letter was informative to say the least. Maxwell Denton was the kid's name. In it, he described his version of the events of the night in question. Maxwell thought he killed the girl, and that he had turned into a werewolf that night. He said he had a habit of sleepwalking. What a wicked letdown. This kid ain't the savage I thought he was. He's a sleepwalker that only conjures up bravery when he's unconscious! I hadn't been that disappointed since they read the decision for the second Gatti-Ward fight.

There had to be something inside him, though. Some form of savagery, buried deep down that I could use to my advantage. I liked to think there was a little "Irish" Mickey Ward that I could bring out of Maxwell, even when he's still awake.

Maxwell ended the letter, saying that he was chaining himself up in the basement. That's where I found him. Chained up, crying, and confused.

"Who are you?" he asked.

"Maxwell Denton?" I replied. "My name is Sawyer Quinn, and I'm about to turn you into the world's fiercest frickin' werewolf hunter."

DARK ASSENT

By E.M. Nelson

The loud buzzing of the alarm fills the room, throbbing through my head like a jackhammer on a stubborn piece of cement. It's been years since I drank so much, and I'm surprised that Kate let me, with it being our fifth anniversary and all. She had made a big fuss about planning a romantic evening at home since Janet, our seven-month-old daughter, is still too young to be away from her for an extended period of time. It's a shame I don't remember more than the first few sips of wine. I'm sure Kate is going to be mad when she realizes it.

Groaning with the effort, I roll over, intent on stopping the noise. It isn't like Kate to let the alarm go off for so long; she's usually up first either feeding the baby or starting the coffee. The edge of the bed is closer than I anticipated, and I fall in a painful heap to the floor. Cursing as I massage my now pounding head, I scramble to stand and slam my hand down on the alarm clock.

While recovering from my abrupt departure from the bed, one thing becomes startlingly apparent, I am balls naked and covered in some sort of sticky liquid that looks brown in the dim light. The smell hits me next, causing me to gag. It is a deep, pungent smell; a mixture of wet dog hair and some metallic base that I can't quite place my finger on. The room is a total disaster; pieces of broken furniture are strewn all over, the white comforter and pillows are smeared in the same disgusting liquid as me, and everything lies in a shredded mess across what's left of the bed.

Rubbing the back of my head, I feel a deep gouge. I definitely didn't hit my head that hard falling off the bed. What the heck happened last night? And where is my wife?

Tossing on a pair of boxers, I cautiously move through the

disaster pile that used to be our bedroom. The door and surrounding walls have deep, claw-like scratches, and it takes me a minute to realize the door handle will not operate, as it has been jammed and apparently broken somehow. Using my shoulder, I slam against the door repeatedly, yelling for Kate. Since I can't remember squat, I'm hoping she'll have some kind of explanation.

The door finally gives way, sending me crashing to the floor in the hallway. Standing, I reach for the light switch and quickly realize the hallway is more messed up than the bedroom. In the light, I realize the sticky stuff that I'm soaked in is also streaked everywhere, and it looks a lot like blood. The bookcase and several chairs from the dining room are also piled up through the hallway.

"Kate?" I call out, a sense of panic growing at the sight of the blood. There is no answer. "Katherine," I yell louder, growing more panicked by the second.

Squeezing past the furniture pile, I follow a trail of blood which leads toward the kitchen. Taking a deep, steadying breath I force myself to walk into the kitchen, not sure of what I'll find there, but fearing the worst. The kitchen looks normal compared to the disaster zone in the rest of the house. The only thing out of place is a deep red trail of blood on the floor which disappears behind the island.

"Katherine?" I call out gently, silently praying to anything that will listen that she'll answer. As calmly as I can, I walk further into the kitchen, a lump building in my throat, threatening to choke me. Rounding the counter, I find Kate lying on the floor surrounded by a large pool of blood. Her eyes are open and stare blankly in my direction. The shredded remains of the yellow dress she had been wearing last night hang limply across her ravaged body. Large, claw-like marks cover her torso and neck. It's hard to tell with all the blood, but it also appears as if a large chunk has been ripped out of her left calf. In the seven and a half years I have worked as a detective for the Philadelphia police, I have never seen anything as disturbing as this.

Falling to my knees, I grab her hand and begin sobbing uncontrollably. What could have done this to my beautiful wife? I've been known to get violent in the past when I've had a few too many, which is why I no longer drink, but I've never done anything like this. What other explanation could there be though? We don't own any pets and, as far as I can remember, we didn't have any guests last night; which leaves only one logical explanation.

My detective side urges me to release my wife, as I am contaminating potential evidence. But the husband in me is screaming back that this is my wife; my perfect, beautiful wife lying cold and dead on the kitchen floor. I'll touch her and hold her as long as I can if it'll do anything to make this nightmare end. I know it won't, but accepting that is incomprehensible. Immense guilt floods through me and I suddenly find it hard to breathe. Even if I had nothing to do with this, which isn't likely, I let her down by not being there to protect her from whatever did. I promised to love her and protect her, and I couldn't even do that. And our daughter… Where is our daughter?

A new sense of panic slashes through me, filling me past the point of what any human should be asked to endure. Gently laying my wife's hand back on her body, I jump to my feet, searching the kitchen for any sign of our daughter, Janet. The house is deadly quiet. Facing the hallway, I notice the barricade of furniture, which is in front of Janet's door. Quickly I move the furniture, piece by blood covered piece, pausing briefly with my hand on the door knob. What if I find something more horrific than I did in the kitchen? Will I ever be able to function normally again? It will break me, but I know that there is no way to get past looking inside the nursery. I have to know if my entire world has been destroyed, or if, by some small piece of luck, there is any hope left for me.

Pushing the door slowly open, I brace myself for whatever is beyond it. The room is bright with the sunlight streaming through the window. Everything is perfectly in place and devoid of any blood, a stark contrast to the rest of the house. A gentle rustling followed by a small coo catches my attention. I rush to the side of the crib and find Janet lying on her back, grabbing her toes and smiling happily at the giraffe painted on the wall above her. Relief washes through me, leaving me nearly too weak to stand. Gripping the side of her crib, I look down at her smiling face. If she is frightened by the sight of me, she doesn't show it. Instead, she sticks out her tongue, blowing raspberries at me before rolling back toward the giraffe. A single, heavy tear rolls down my blood covered cheek, falling to the white sheet below, staining it dark red.

Assured that Janet is safe, I know the only thing left to do is to call the precinct and notify them of the incident. The first few hours after a crime are the most crucial, and every move I make in my home, the crime scene, has the possibility of disrupting the evidence. I don't want to believe it, but I know there is a chance this whole thing is my fault. Gently, I scoop Janet out of her crib, holding her away from my chest to minimize the amount of blood I get on her, and return to the kitchen.

Grabbing the cordless house phone, I place the baby in her highchair and stand in front of her, blocking her view of her mother. She might be a baby, but I don't want her to have to see any part of what has happened if I can avoid it. She smiles happily at me as I dial the emergency number and continues to as the phone rings several times before an automated message comes on from the emergency broadcast system.

"We apologize for the delay. Due to the high number of calls being routed through our call center, we are experiencing longer than normal wait times. If this is a life-threatening emergency, please contact your local emergency room, or personal physician."

"What the heck?" I end the call and dial the number once more. The recording comes on after the first ring, and I disconnect the call before it can get through the first sentence. Janet squeals unhappily, reminding me how dire my situation truly is. Cursing under my breath, I pick her up with my free arm and bounce her gently in an attempt to soothe her while I get someone on the line.

Since the emergency number isn't working, I decide to try my partner, detective Dereck Marshall. We cover a different district, but I know he will be able to help me get someone here to help take care of the situation. His phone rings through to voicemail. Grabbing my phone list off the fridge, I try every number from dispatch to my boss, each call going unanswered. Running out of other options, I dial the number I have for Clark and Dianna, Kate's parents. The phone rings three times, and I am about to hang up when a soft, shaky voice answers.

"Hello?"

"Thank you," I sigh, grateful to have anyone answer. "Dianna? This is Steve."

"Uh, no," the frail sounding voice whispers. "This is Kim, her daughter."

"Kim, it's Steve," I say. "I need to talk to your dad."

"Um," she says, choking back sobs. "He can't... I just... they're... it's... it's... it's..."

"Kimberly," I say as calmly as I can. "What's wrong? Where's Clark? Can you get your mom?"

"They're dead," she finally whispers between sobs.

"Okay, Kimberly, what happened?" I ask, trying to sound reassuring. "Are you alright?"

"Those things got them," she cries out. "Just like the girls in my dorm last night. What am I supposed to do Steve?"

"What things are you talking about? Is there someone in the house?"

"No, I don't know what they are," she whispers. "They were everywhere last night."

"Have you called the police yet?" I ask, though I fear I know what her answer will be before she gives it.

"I tried, but no one is answering."

I'm not sure what is going on there, or what things she's talking about, but if my in-laws are dead and there was an attack at her dorm, then there is a chance that all of this, including whatever happened to my wife, is somehow connected. Every possible explanation races through my mind. Could it have been an attempt at killing the whole family? As an attorney working for the state, Clark does have several people who would want him dead, but that wouldn't explain the other deaths. It could also be some random coincidence. Either way, I know that the safest place for Kim, and the best way to try and piece as much of the evidence together as I can, is for her to come to me.

"Okay, listen carefully to me Kimberly. I need you to lock up your parent's house and come here to the apartment. Can you do that for me?"

She doesn't respond.

"Kimberly?"

"Yes," she whispers.

"Can you do that?"

"Yes."

"Good. Go now then. Don't touch anything but the door, and make sure you lock the deadbolt. In traffic, it should only take you fifteen minutes tops to get here. If you run into any trouble, you call me here on our house phone okay?"

"Okay," she breathes shakily, and disconnects the call.

Setting the phone down on the table, I stare at it with the thoughts running through my head of all the things I need to do once we can get someone from 911 on the line. Janet begins fussing, pushing away from me as hard as she can, bringing my focus back to the more pressing need of caring for her.

"Hungry?" I ask, setting her back in the highchair. She wails in reply, kicking her legs and arching her back in an attempt to escape the chair.

Turning her toward the fridge, I take one of the small bags of frozen breast milk from the freezer and prepare it. Once it is warmed, I grab her from the highchair, taking her back to her crib and propping the bottle up in her mouth with a stuffed animal. It may not be the best form of parenting, but I need her safely out of the way.

After getting Janet settled, I hurry to the master bathroom to clean myself up. I'm going to have to break the news to Kim about Kate when she gets here, but I don't want her to see me covered in her sister's blood. Taking the time to photograph myself both front and back for evidence, I quickly wash in the shower and toss on the cleanest pair of clothes I am able to find in my bedroom. I'm just finishing buttoning my shirt when the bell rings.

The look on Kim's face when I open the door makes me glad I didn't tell her about Kate over the phone. She is clearly in shock from everything, and I know that when I tell her what has happened it will break her.

"Where's Kate?" She blurts out suddenly, staring into my eyes like she can see my soul. I look down, unable to bear my own grief, let alone the deeper pain I see burning within her.

A darkness enters her voice. "She's gone too, isn't she?"

I nod, heavy tears streaming unbidden down my cheeks. I am unable to speak and unsure of what I would say if I could.

"How could you let that happen?" She screeches at me, pounding my chest with her fists. "How could you not save her?"

Grabbing her hands, I pull her to me, hugging her tight to my chest. It's partly to stop her assault and partly to try and quell the ache that is throbbing deep in my soul. She's right to be angry with me, and a small part of me wishes that she could hit me harder, hard enough to make me forget the pain, hard enough to kill me so I will never have to feel the pain again. She won't, of course, and the logical part of my brain whispers that I am still needed by my daughter, but if it would right what has been done, I would gladly die a million times over.

"I'm so sorry Kim," I whisper into her hair. Clinging to my shirt, she sobs into my chest. I wish I had some explanation to offer her, some way to make it all make sense, but I don't, and I know that any explanation or theory I could come up with would never make any of it right.

"The world's gone crazy and I don't know what to do," she cries, clinging to me harder than before. "Tell me what I'm supposed to do."

"We'll call the precinct again," I offer, trying to sound soothing despite my emotions. "They'll send someone out to help us figure out who did this."

Shoving herself out of my arms, she looks at me incredulously. "Don't you get it, Steve? There is no one at the precinct, no one will answer when you call, and no one will come. Everything is messed up out there, and we're all alone!"

"What are you talking about?" I ask, confused.

"Seriously Steve?" She pushes past me and begins walking to the balcony door. "Have you even looked outside today?"

"I'm sorry; I was a little preoccupied with finding my wife dead on the kitchen floor." I reply, following her into the apartment, my voice more terse than I mean for it to be. "Staring out the window didn't exactly cross my mind."

"Does this look normal to you?" she asks, shoving the curtains aside and gesturing for me to join her.

The street below us is in utter chaos. Cars are stopped at random angles in the road. Windows on the lower levels of the building across the street are broken. The sidewalks are covered in trash and streaks of an ominous red substance. It is unreal, like a scene from a movie.

"What happened?" I ask, looking to Kim for answers.

"What do you mean 'What happened'? Those things, the ones that got Kate and my parents, they happened." She stares at me like what she's said should clue me in to some grand explanation.

"What things?"

"Those big wolf-things," she says, shaking her head at me. "Seriously Steve, look around your house; it's pretty clear one of them got in here."

"A wolf?" I frown. A wolf could explain the scratches on the walls, and the bite marks on Kate's body, but how would a wolf get into our third-floor apartment in the middle of Philadelphia?

"Really?" She yells, clearly getting exasperated with me. "Did you sleep through the whole thing or something?"

I look down at my hands and then back up at her, noticing for the first time that she has scratches on both her face and arms, while I have none. "I don't remember much of last night." I admit. "Kate made dinner, and I remember having a few sips of wine… then it all goes blank."

"You're kidding me, right? You fought it off or got knocked out trying to save her didn't you? Or maybe you..."

"I don't remember anything else." I cut her off angrily.

I'm already frustrated about not remembering the night before and I don't need her adding to that. Guilt hits me instantly. She's lost just as much today as me. Rubbing the bridge of my nose, I take a deep breath. Getting angry with her isn't going to solve anything.

"I'm sorry. It's just been a lot to deal with today, ya know? I'm trying my best with everything that's going on. Let's start again. What were you saying about wolves?"

"They're not wolves. I mean, they looked like wolves, but much, much bigger." Her eyes grow wide as she speaks, her breath quickening.

"So you saw these large wolves attack people?"

She nods. "I was in the hallway at my dorm when it happened. My roommate and I were just heading out to go to dinner with some friends. I forgot my purse, so she was at the other end of the hall when I came out. One second she was standing there, talking to the girls in 2B, and the next a huge wolf-thing ripped out of her skin. Everything went crazy. She... IT attacked the other girls and I ran back in our room and barricaded the door. Look, I know you think I'm crazy," she folds her arms tightly across her chest. "But I swear that's what I saw."

I stare at her, unsure of how to respond. It could be that shock has pushed her over the edge mentally and she made this up to protect herself from accepting the truth. I've seen it before at work. Someone deeply affected by a tragedy starts making up all sorts of possible explanations for the situation and they cling to them, hoping for a more normal outcome.

"It's not that I think you're crazy," I finally say, trying to remember what the grief counselors usually do for people like this. "I just think there has to be some kind of a more logical explanation."

"A more logical explanation?" She shrieks, storming over to the TV and turning it on to one of the news stations. "Look at this and tell me that there is any kind of logical explanation that you could come up with to explain it."

Chaotic scenes fill the screen. People covered in blood, running, screaming, being pursued by large, wolf-like animals. "... like a nightmare come to life," the newscaster says. "We are still unsure of the total casualty count, but initial numbers indicate that more than half of the population has been affected at this time."

"What in the world?" I ask, dumbfounded by what I see on the TV. The images are so unbelievable I would think it was a hoax if my wife wasn't lying in the other room with very similar wounds to those they are showing on the screen. An idea of what must have happened last night slowly starts forming in my head, and I'm not sure I like where it is going.

"See, I'm not crazy," Kim says.

The picture changes to a graphic map of the nation. "Despite the severity of the situation, no reports of any of what some are deeming as 'werewolf activity' have been reported from outside the U.S. It seems that it is, so far, an isolated event." The image changes to show the young reporter. "We are just now receiving word that Canada's Prime Minister is expected to speak later today concerning the closing of the Canada/ United States border. We'll keep you updated as that information becomes available. This move to close the border comes in light of a mass exodus of both U.S. and natural Canadian citizens, in hopes of reaching what some are calling a safe haven. The border remains open for now, but that is expected to change once the Prime Minister speaks following the emergency session of Parliament currently being held."

Tearing my eyes away from the screen, I turn to Kim. "We have to go there, now."

"Go where?" She frowns. "To Canada?" I nod.

"Why would we do that? We could just hunker down here and wait until the government figures things out."

"No, Kim, we can't. Don't you realize what all this means?" I ask, but before she can answer Janet cries out.

Kim's eyes light up in an unexpected way. "She's alive?"

I nod, and without hesitation she turns and goes down the

hallway to the nursery. Seeing Janet cradled in the arms of her aunt, who looks so much like my wife that they were often mistaken as twins, widens the gouge in my heart and steals my breath. My soul aches to see her held in my wife's arms again. Kim gently nuzzles Janet, making her giggle, something my wife used to do, and I find myself almost completely unhinged. Unable to stop them, tears begin streaming down my face. Trying to control my emotions, I turn away from them both.

"Steve," Kim whispers behind me, and I can tell from her voice that she too is crying. "Thank you."

Wiping my eyes on my sleeve, I turn back to her, forcing a smile that I don't really feel. "For what?"

"For saving her. For keeping this one small piece of Kate alive."

"There's no reason to thank me," I say hoarsely. "I told you already that I don't remember anything from last night."

"Whether you remember it or not, I'm sure you did everything you could to keep her safe,"

I shake my head. "Look Kim, the thing is…" I trail off, not sure how to put into words what I have to say. "The thing is I'm almost certain I'm the one who killed Kate. I can't explain it, but I think I've known deep down all morning that it was me, but it didn't sink in until I saw those things on the news."

She doesn't respond. Her piercing gaze just stays locked with mine, burrowing its way through me. I fidget uncomfortably, waiting for an explosive reaction. Clinging to Janet, she takes a slow step back from me. A slap to the face would have stung less.

"I'm not going to hurt you, or her," I say, holding my hands out.

"How can I trust you when you just admitted to killing my sister?"

"I didn't admit to it," I shake my head. "I can't admit to

something I don't remember. I'm just saying it seems pretty obvious with how things are around here that it was me that did it. I mean, how else would one of those things have gotten in here and killed her, but left me alone in the bed? There are claw marks on the walls of the room I woke up locked in for heaven's sake. It's pretty damning evidence, wouldn't you say?"

She swallows hard. "So what are we supposed to do then?"

Perhaps it is from my years on the force, or possibly my own disconnect from the situation due to all the emotional trauma I've endured, but I find myself overcome with a strange sort of calm. I can clearly see what must be done, and though I regret the way I'll have to leave things here, I know that this is the only way to assure that my wife didn't die in vain.

"We have to try and get you both across the border to Canada," I say matter-of-factly.

"What good is that going to do? At least here we have a place to stay, food to eat. If we go there, we won't have any security at all."

"It will be safer for you there. You heard the lady on the news, this was limited to the United States. Canada was unaffected."

Hugging the baby tighter to her chest, she backs further away from me. "What if you're wrong?" She asks. "What if it happens there? I can't go through that again."

"It won't. I promise. Look," I plead. "We'll stop before nightfall and hide in a hotel or something. We can find somewhere safe to be until morning. Those creatures only seem to come out at night so it'll work. It has to."

She shakes her head slowly, still unwilling to come closer. "How do you know they'll even let us across the border?"

"I don't," I sigh, dropping my hands. "But I have to try. I can't just stay here pretending nothing happened. If there's any chance to guarantee Janet's safety, I have to take it."

"And if they don't let us cross? What then? At least here we know we could be safe."

"For how long though Kim? How long do you think you'd last with a baby in a city that has been affected this badly?" My voice rises with frustration. "I can't make you come with us, but I have to try. For her sake," I nod at the baby. "Kate would want her to be safe, you know that."

She stares at me silently for several long seconds. "Fine," she says, tears welling in her eyes again. "I'll go, but it's only because it's what Kate would have wanted."

After clearing out the cabinets of any easily prepared food, I load it and the last of the frozen milk into a box and take it to the car. Avoiding the kitchen at all costs, Kim packs a bag of baby supplies and buckles Janet into her car seat. It takes us less than twenty minutes to get everything loaded. As we pull away from the building, my heart feels like it has been ripped in half.

The streets are devoid of any life, but despite the cars and other debris, the roads are relatively easy to navigate. Once we hit the highway, the number of obstacles drops considerably and we are able to drive at normal speeds. Kim stares out the window, clearly trying to avoid having to talk to me. I can't blame her. I'm unsure of what to say, but the silence that stretches between us reverberates until I feel like I am going to lose my mind. With nothing else to focus on, my brain keeps replaying the events of the morning. It is all I can do to stay focused enough to drive.

Switching the radio on, I search for a station with some kind of music, or news, or anything to listen to that will give me something other than my wife to think about. All of the preset stations are playing a crackling static, so I set it to scan. After searching for several silent minutes, it stops on a lone station playing a public service announcement.

"…residents are urged to remain inside until further instructions

169

can be given." A mechanical sounding woman's voice drones. "Local authorities have declared Martial Law for the entire state of Pennsylvania. Due to the recent attacks, travel has been restricted within the state, and residents are urged to remain inside until further instructions can be given."

The message plays over and over, on a permanent repeat. Reaching forward, I turn the stereo off, avoiding looking at Kim, who has turned towards me with what I know must be a look of fear.

"We're not going to keep going are we?" She asks, leaning towards me.

I nod, still avoiding her gaze. "We have to."

"Steve, if they've declared Martial Law, we could be shot if we're caught out on the roads."

"Shot by who? Look around, there's no one left to enforce any of the laws."

"But what if…"

"We're not going back," I cut her off, ending the discussion. Falling back into an uncomfortable silence, we continue on, each of us battling our own demons while Janet, blissfully unaware of the whole situation, sleeps soundly in the backseat.

Despite the public service announcement, the first sign of life we encounter is a barricade on one of the off ramps. A large sign hooked to the hastily erected chain link fence reads 'Wolf-free zone. Trespassers will be shot on sight.' As we pass, Kim points out several men, who appear to be armed to the teeth with weapons, ready to enforce the warning on the sign. While I am wary of what this could mean for the rest of our journey, I also find myself envious of their situation. Under different circumstances, I would have attempted something similar to help protect my family. We pass through the area without any incident.

Halfway across New Jersey the gas light blinks on. "You've got to be kidding me," I whisper harshly, hitting my hand against the edge of the steering wheel. If I had just remembered to fill up when Kate asked me to, we would have made it much farther before having to do this.

Weaving around several mangled cars, I pull off the next exit. Driving slower than necessary, I pull into the first gas station we encounter. The windows of the building are intact, which is a heartening sight after all the destruction we have seen.

"Stay here and keep the doors locked," I say, putting the car in park and unbuckling my seatbelt. "I'm going to go check and see if anyone's in there."

"I don't know about this Steve," Kim says nervously.

"Trust me, ok?" She nods, though I can tell by the look in her eyes that she is scared to death. Taking a deep, bracing breath I step out of the car and shut the door, waiting next to it until I hear Kim hit the button to engage the locks. The silence of the neighborhood is deafening. Walking slowly, I try to peer through the windows to see if anyone is at the register, but the tinting makes it hard to tell. As I push the door open, a wave of hot air rushes out, enveloping me in its pungent odor. I am instantly reminded of the smell that filled my apartment this morning, and it quickly becomes clear that anyone who had been in the building didn't survive the night. Having had more than enough gory scenes for the day, I retreat back outside.

Nodding to Kim to let her know that everything is okay, I quickly unscrew the gas cap and begin fueling the car. I feel guilty for stealing the gas, but I know that without it I have no chance at getting my daughter to safety.

Before the tank has time to fill completely, a loud clanging across the street draws my attention. Heart racing, I peer around to see if I can identify what made the noise, but don't see anyone or anything. Unnerved by the sound, I quickly replace the nozzle and climb into the car, locking the doors behind me.

"Was there anyone in there?" Kim asks.

"No," I lie. The haunted look on her face says she doesn't believe me, but she doesn't say anything else. After buckling in, I start the car and put it in drive. The tank is only three-quarters of the way full, but I was too nervous to fill it completely up. As we begin pulling out of the parking lot, there is a flurry of movement in the building across the street. In an instant, a group of raggedly dressed people come rushing out, waving weapons and yelling loudly. The hair on the back of my neck stands on end. It isn't words but howls, like those a wolf would make.

"Go Steve," Kim screams as the mob rushes towards us.

Without hesitation, I floor the gas pedal, swerving around the first of the group, who are nearly close enough to touch the car. A baseball bat smashes against the driver's side mirror, ripping it off. Keeping the pedal pressed all the way down, we speed back the way we came, slowing only enough to safely get back onto the freeway without hitting any of the other cars.

Glancing in the rearview mirror frequently to check for any followers, we speed much faster than the posted signs. Kim crawls into the backseat to distract herself with caring for Janet. She warms a bottle for her with the heater since we have no other options at the moment. We make good time, covering what should have been a five-hour drive in just under four. The gas light blinks on again just as we're entering a town near the Canadian border. I'm nervous to fill up again after what happened at the last gas station, but I'm not sure if my American dollars will be good once we cross into Canada. I need enough gas in the tank to get us as far from the border as possible. Cautiously, I select the gas station in the most open area and pull up to the pump.

"I'm not ready to do this again," Kim says, visibly shaking.

"It'll be okay," I reassure her. "I'll leave it running while I fill it, and if anything looks out of place, we'll leave."

"You make it sound so simple," she sighs, rubbing her hands over her face.

"It will be," I say, opening the door.

A dusty breeze blows past me as I open the gas cap and fit the nozzle in. As I fill the tank, I glance around checking for any signs of life. It looks just as dead here as it did at the last station, but I know how quickly that could change. This gas station is an older looking business, with pumps that appear to be from the 1950's. Except for the bloody sidewalks, it's like pulling into a postcard.

The nozzle clicks, and I remove it from the car, shaking it off. A familiar mechanical click behind me curdles the blood in my veins. Very slowly I turn around. An older man with grey hair and weather worn skin stands in the doorway of the gas station with a shotgun pointed directly at me.

"You plan on pay'n for that?" He asks with an out of place southern drawl.

"Yes sir," I say, holding my hands up in front of me. "I just need to grab my wallet from the car."

"Why don't ya just have that purdy lady in there hand it to ya son?" He suggests, stepping towards me. "Not that I don't trust ya, but I can't be too cautious these days."

Slowly opening the door, I hold my hand out to Kim. "I need my wallet," I say as casually as possible.

"What's going on?" She whispers, fumbling around in the console to grab it for me.

"I just have to pay for the gas," I say loud enough for the man behind me to hear, then quietly whisper, "Lock the doors and be ready to leave if this goes bad."

She nods and hits the lock button as soon as I shut the door.

Turning back to the man, I dig out a wad of cash and hold it out to him. "How much do I owe you?"

"Well the pump says sixty dollars son, so that's what I'll take. I'm no crook, I won't try'n cheat ya outa yer hard earned money." he says, lowering the gun. I quickly count out the sixty and hand it to him.

"Thank ya fer yer business." He nods his head at me, holding the cash up in a salute. I smile politely and turn back to the car. "If ya don't mind me askin', where y'all headed?" His question stops me mid-stride.

Plastering on a smile, I turn back towards him. "We were headed to see some family." I lie.

"Ah, they live here in Champlain?"

"No, uh, they're up in Montreal." I say, rubbing my palms gently against my pant legs.

"I see. Well good luck crossing the border. We just heard from another fellah that stopped by here a bit ago, that they might've shut the border down 'til all this mess can get figured out."

"Shut it down completely?" I ask, my stomach knotting up at the thought of what that will mean for us.

"That's what he said," he nods.

"Is there any chance of getting across somewhere else?"

"Not legally son. You in some kind of trouble? Or just tryin' to get away from all this madness goin' on here?"

I shake my head, glancing back at the car. "I just want to get my daughter safely across the border."

"And check on yer family up there in Canada right?"

"Yeah, of course," I agree, remembering the lie. "We've just come so far, and it'll be night soon..." I trail off, realizing I was about to tell a perfect stranger, who is holding a shotgun in his hands, that I am more than likely a werewolf.

He nods. "Well, best of luck to ya son. If ya don't get across the border, Missy n' I own a little bed n' breakfast and we'd love to have y'all as guests. It's the safest place you'll get after dark, ya know just in case those things come back." His smile is genuine, easing a little of my anxiety.

"Thank you," I say, sliding into the driver's seat. "I'll keep that in mind."

He waves us off as we pull out of the parking lot. We sit in silence until we are safely back on the road. "What was that all about?" She asks once we turn the corner.

"He was just offering a place to stay in case we didn't make it across the border."

"Why wouldn't we make it across? Is there something he knows that we don't?"

"We'll make it," I assure her, though I'm not entirely sure how we're going to do that if the border is indeed closed.

The freeway leading to the border is deserted, making me feel nervous. Arriving at the crossing, the feeling of unease begins to swell, bordering full on panic. Large cement blockades have been placed in rows across the road, barbed wire trails as far as the eye can see in either direction, and armored military vehicles are spaced periodically along the fence. Slowing the car, I pull up to the edge of the blockade and stop. A guard, dressed in a heavy layer of protective gear, steps out of the vehicle on the opposite side and raises his weapon. Cautiously, I open the door and step out of the car.

"Return to your vehicle immediately," the guard yells, indicating with his gun. "The border has been closed and is in the process of being sealed. No one is permitted access."

"Please," I beg, holding my hands up. "I have a baby. Just let her cross..."

"Return to your vehicle now," the man continues, ignoring my plea. "Or I will use lethal force."

"I can pay..."

The soldier cocks the slide, silencing further protestation. Moving quickly, I slide back into the car and shut the door. I will be no help to anyone dead. Kim is sobbing in the back seat, staring down the barrel of the gun that is now pointed at the car. Unsure of what to do next, I know that sitting here having a stare-down with the Canadian military is useless. Executing one of the swiftest three point turns in my history of driving, I speed back up the freeway.

"What do we do now?" Kim cries.

"I don't know."

"Can we cross the border somewhere else?"

"I don't know," I say, gripping the wheel tighter.

"It's almost dark; what are we going to do? We're hours away from home, and we don't have anywhere to go, or anything to defend ourselves with. What if those things come back? What if you change into one of them? I can't go through that again," she wails, her voice rising with each panic filled word.

"Stop, Kim," I say, using every fiber of my self-control to keep from yelling.

"But what if-"

"I said stop," I bellow, cutting her off. Janet cries out, startled from my shouting.

Kim leans forward, her face just inches from my elbow. "We have to do something, Steve, it'll be dark soon."

I sigh, feeling like a jerk for yelling at her. "I know."

"We could always go back to that gas station. Didn't the guy there say he had a place we could stay?"

"Yeah," I nod. "But I don't know if we can trust him."

"It's better than nothing," she says, sitting back and consoling Janet.

Deciding to listen to her for once instead of disregarding her ideas, we return to the gas station. It is just as deserted looking as last time and for a second I'm afraid that the old man might have left for the day, but then I see movement in the window and recognize the pattern on the shirt that he was wearing. Kim clutches Janet to her while I carry the diaper bag and we head into the store.

"That didn't take long," the old man says, pulling chips from a box and arranging them on the shelf.

I scratch the back of my head. "Yeah, I guess that other guy was right. The border is closed."

"Well that's a shame." He glances over at us from where he is stocking the shelf. "Anything I can do to help ya?"

"You had mentioned that you owned a bed and breakfast earlier..." I trail off, feeling slightly uncomfortable at having to take advantage of a stranger's hospitality.

He nods. "Sure do. The wife'd love ta have guests too. Lemme just finish up with this and I'll take ya over there."

"Thank you," I say, though it doesn't feel like enough to express my gratitude.

"Don't think anything of it," he says, grabbing his keys and setting the empty box on the counter. "Missy loves havin' guests and what with all this nonsense goin' on, I'm sure it'll be a while before we get a chance to have anyone stop by again. Besides it's been far too long since we had anyone as cute as that little lady stay with us." He nods at Janet, who is happily smiling at him.

"Thank you," Kim says, waving Janet's hand for her.

"You can stay with us as long as ya need." He leads us out the back door of the store and across the street to a small, two-story house. "My name's Patrick, by the way. Not sure if I introduced myself properly or not yet."

"Thank you for your hospitality Patrick," I say, eyeing the house warily, a sense of guilt building in me. What if Kim was right and I change again tonight? I wouldn't be able to live with myself if I unwittingly injured anyone else, especially an innocent elderly couple. I stay put on the sidewalk as he hobbles up onto the porch, opening the door for us.

"Look," I lick my lips nervously, glancing over at Kim. "I have to be straight with you. I woke up this morning with no memory of last night to find that my wife had been killed..." I trail off, not physically able to get through telling him everything that happened.

"I won't judge ya son," he smiles gently at me. "There are some things in life that we just can't control, don't beat yourself up over it," he pushes the door open further. "You're still welcome to stay with us until you can figure things out if you'd like."

"I appreciate that," I nod, stepping towards him. "But I'd hate to put you in any kind of danger, if it happens again tonight. And I need to be sure my family is safe and taken care of first, just in case it does."

"I understand your need to get your family somewhere safe. I'm a father too and I'd do the same thing if I was in your shoes. I might be able to help you out with that. Why don't you come in for some dinner and we can discuss it while we eat?"

Reluctantly, I accept his offer. He gives us a quick tour of the house, pointing out the rooms we can use if we choose to stay for the night, before taking us into the kitchen. It is old and worn but in a homely, comfortable way. He then introduces his wife, Missy, who is hard at work preparing a salad to accompany a homemade pot pie steaming on the stove top. Though I'm anxious to discuss the help he mentioned, I don't want to be rude, so I wait until after dinner before bringing it up.

"Our son Jeffery works as a border guard over there in Canada," he explains as we help clear the table. "He married a Canadian national several years ago and decided that livin' up there with her family was what they needed, so they moved up there and he got himself a job with the Canadian Border Services Agency. We go up 'n' visit him every couple of weeks."

"So he works for the actual border patrol?" I ask.

He nods. "Sure does. He's the supervising agent for this area too. Now I can't guarantee anythin', but when Missy called to check up on him earlier, he mentioned he'd be in the area tonight. We were plannin' on takin' him some dinner, and if you happened to tag along, I might be able to talk him into helpin' y'all get across the border."

"That would be amazing," I say, looking at Kim. She doesn't look as excited about it as me, but with night fast approaching and the likelihood of me turning into a wolf again unknown, it's the best news I've heard all day.

We spend the next half hour discussing the plan. Patrick explains that he thinks it will be the safest option for him to talk to his son alone, while we wait in the car. That way he can explain our situation in a non-threatening way, and his son won't feel pressured to agree to anything if he isn't able to help. We agree, having no other options open to us, and pile into the back of his car for the ride to the border.

Every muscle in my body tenses as Patrick approaches the guard alone when we arrive at the border. He nods and motions at the car. Though I can't hear what he is saying, I can tell from his body language that he is explaining our situation. The guard looks over at the car then back at Patrick, nods once, then turns and walks over to his tank. Several tense minutes pass before he returns. When he does, he hands Patrick a sheet of paper and points towards us. Patrick shakes his head and they continue talking.

After what feels like forever, the guard finally reaches out and they shake hands. Patrick turns and motions for us to join them, and

I slowly exit the car, waiting for Kim as she grabs Janet. As we approach, a second guard walks up, handcuffs in hand. It throws me off a bit, though I guess I should have expected that they wouldn't allow a suspected werewolf to just walk freely across the border unrestrained. Taking a deep breath, I square my shoulders and hold my head high. This is the best thing for my family, and I will do what I must to assure their safety.

"Mr. Shipman?" the guard asks, stepping towards me.

"Yes, sir."

"We've been informed that you wish to willingly participate in the World United Anti-Werewolf Movement, is that correct?"

I frown, glancing at Patrick. "I'm not sure what that is…"

"It's a program that will allow you to cross the border, in exchange for a couple of… tests to help in determining what caused the incident last night."

"And my family will be safe?"

"Of course," Patrick says, patting me on the shoulder.

"Do you wish to willingly participate?" the guard asks again.

I rub my neck uncomfortably. Patrick never said anything about tests but if that's what it'll take to get us across the border, then I have no choice but to accept. "Yeah, sure," I nod.

"You understand the ramifications of this decision and willingly agree to comply with all that is asked of you?" the guard asks.

"As long as my family is safe, I don't care what happens to me." I say, looking him directly in the eyes. He smiles half-heartedly and glances over at Patrick again, one eyebrow raised. Patrick ignores him, keeping his eyes on me, and I can't help but think I'm missing something.

"Sign here, giving your consent to continue," the guard says, holding out a pen and paper which is covered in fine print that is too small to read from this distance. Hesitantly, I grab the paper and hold it closer to my face as I try to read it. I was never any good with English in school and the large words used on the document are, if nothing else, confusing to me.

The gist of the first paragraph includes a description of why the governing forces have decided to found the movement, which I can understand pretty well, but then it starts talking about legal ramifications and medical procedures I've never heard of and my understanding begins slipping away. The guard clears his throat impatiently and Patrick pats my shoulder again, looking down at his watch. "It'll be dark soon," he hints. Naturally he's right, and heaven only knows what it'll mean for me if I change again.

Swallowing hard, I grab the pen and sign on the line. The guard nods once, signaling his comrade to step forward. He places the handcuffs on me, securing them tighter than necessary, and pushes me towards the tank. A second armored vehicle pulls up near the tank and three large soldiers step out, each of them carrying an arsenal of weapons and looking like they could kill me with their bare hands if those failed. As they approach, Patrick turns and starts walking back to his car. The soldiers grab Kim, ripping Janet from her arms, and handcuff her in a rough manner.

"Wait, I thought you said they'd be safe if I turned myself in," I shout to Patrick's retreating back. He continues walking, acting like he never heard me. A mixture of panic and despair tear through me at the realization of what he's done. Tugging at the handcuffs, I try to pull away from the guard. When that fails to gain me any ground I begin begging.

"Please let them go," I cry. "You have me, I'll come freely I promise, just let them go." My pleas fall on deaf ears though, and the man continues dragging me away.

I watch in horror as the other guards shove Kim in the back of their vehicle and climb in behind her, holding my daughter. The sight of him holding her pushes me past the edge and in a surge of adrenaline I tear away from the guard holding me. Barreling towards the vehicle containing the last of my reasons to live, I close the distance in a matter of seconds. Though I caught the soldier off guard, he recovers quickly and tackles me from behind just as I reach the truck. My face slams into the ground and blackness wraps itself around my consciousness.

When I wake, I find myself shackled to a bed in a room lit only by the light filtering in through a small, circular window in the ceiling. My head is pounding, and my body feels like it has been hit by a train. The full gravity of my situation sinks in as I become more aware of my surroundings. Several vials sit on a table next to a series of machines, each covered in wires and tubes. The testing that the soldier at the border mentioned must be a real thing. Though I had felt prepared to accept whatever testing they might have in mind for me; that was before they took Kim and Janet into custody too.

Sudden movement to my right catches my attention. A man in a long, white lab coat is seated near the corner of the room, clipboard in hand, staring toward me. I hadn't noticed him immediately when I first woke up due to the low levels of light in the room and the way the shadows make him seemingly blend into the wall. Seeing him now though, I suddenly feel very self-aware. How long has he been watching me? A chill works its way up my neck, causing the hairs on my neck and arms to stand on end.

"Where's my daughter?" I ask. The man doesn't respond; he merely tilts his head to the side, then reaches out and switches on the lights, instantly blinding me. I let out a string of curses, squeezing my eyes shut against the burning light. I can hear him moving around the room and I blink through the pain until my eyes can get fully adjusted to the light, not wanting him to have any greater advantage on me.

He moves from one machine to the next, flipping switches and turning dials, completely ignoring me. It's disconcerting, and yet I feel it should have been expected for him to act this way; I am, after all, a suspected werewolf. Silently, I continue to watch him as he makes his way to each of the machines, making notes after each adjustment on the clipboard in his hands. I wonder if I'm giving them what they want. After what feels like hours, he turns to me and in a curt, nasal voice asks, "Mister Shipman, are you ready to begin?" He doesn't wait for an answer. He moves to the machine closest to me and grabs a handful of wires, and I know that even if I had said no he would have continued anyways.

Once he has attached the wires to several spots on my arms and legs, he moves to my head and, with a firmer grip than I am expecting, turns it so he can attach some to my neck and scalp. Though not comfortable, I barely feel each of the wires touching my body. He tugs on each wire after attaching it, probably checking to make sure it has attached correctly, before moving on to the next. When the final wire is attached, he returns to the machine and hits several switches. It buzzes to life, the entire front of it lighting up like a Christmas tree.

"Let's begin," he says, hitting a button on a small, black rectangle next to him. "Electron test phase one, level one. The subject, a Mister Steven Jay Shipman, claims to have no memories of his change. He willingly submitted himself to be tested and is now entering stage one of the testing cycle."

As soon as he is done speaking, he reaches over and flips a switch. A strange prickling sensation begins humming through my body, emanating from each of the tiny wires. It feels similar to the tingling you get when your foot falls asleep, only all over my body, and much more intense. Resisting the urge to scream, I clench my jaw and breathe heavily through my nose, arching my back away from the bed in a futile attempt at relieving some of the pain. It only lasts a few minutes, but it feels like a lifetime. Just as my vision begins to swim, he turns it off. I collapse against the bed, panting from the strain.

"The subject displays no outward signs of change activated by the test," the man says, making more notes on his clipboard. "While his heart rate did increase dramatically through the test, he displayed no other effects. We shall proceed to phase one of the other tests before continuing on to phase two of the electron test." He hits another button on the black rectangle.

Setting his clipboard on one of the tables, he picks up a long, shiny, pen-like object and walks slowly toward me. At least I think he's walking slowly. My brain is still buzzing from the minor electrocution he just subjected me to, and I'm not sure I can rely on my senses completely anymore. Giving the restraints on my right arm a hard tug, he removes the end of the object in his hands revealing a long, thick needle. My stomach flips at the sight of it; I haven't ever been a fan of needles. He has no trouble locating a vein; they are all sticking out from my arm like tiny traitors, freely giving him access to stab me. With a sharp pinch, he inserts it swiftly and injects whatever concoction he has into me. At first my arm is cold as the liquid mixes into my blood, then the burning starts.

I am unable to contain my screams this time. It literally feels like someone has lit the inside of each of my veins on fire. As it burns its way through my body, I pray for unconsciousness or death; I don't care anymore as long as the pain will stop. I'm not granted either, forced to suffer through the entire process. I can hear him talking through my screams, though his words seem to slur together in my mind, making him sound funny.

I'm not sure when the pain begins to go away, but eventually I find it easier to endure. The burning slowly recedes, leaving me feeling empty and drained. The room is quiet now; the man in the lab coat has gone, probably disgusted with the sight of a grown man screaming like that. I feel no shame in my reaction though; I'm certain it would have done no less to a man twice my size. Now that I am able to fully process what has happened, I am afraid of what is to come.

A door to my left opens and several scientists in white coats enter, talking and laughing like it's the most normal thing in the world to have a man lying half naked on their table being tortured. A shrill scream echoes in through the open door and I recognize it at once as Janet's cry of pain. The last person through the door shuts it, cutting off the sound. Yanking against my bonds, I yell out in a primal way, screaming and pleading for them to let her go. None of them acknowledge me, going about their business like I am beneath their notice. I thrash until every ounce of my energy is gone and then fall back against the bed, wailing like an injured animal, too weak to protest when they draw my blood and begin running the next phase of tests.

I am barely fazed by the things they do to me now, not caring how painful it is for me anymore, now that I know they are hurting her in some way. My tears dry up with what I assume is the tenth test; I've lost count of what one they're on through the endless hours of pain.

A second week passes, each day filled with the next level of tests, and though I listen intently, I never hear Janet's cries again. That, more than anything else they have done, eats at me, making me wish I could just give them what they want so they will allow me to die. The tests have no effect other than the pain, which I bear silently now, accepting it as punishment for what I have done to not only my wife, but now also my daughter and Kim.

The days begin to blur together. Where they were once defined by a break in the pain overnight, the scientists have become aggressive, keeping me up around the clock with new cycles of their tests. The only thing that lets me know time is passing is the tiny window above me, which offers me something to focus on through the pain. It feels as if they have become desperate for some reason. I could ask why, but I doubt I'd get an answer. The pain has reached all new levels, whether from my lack of sleep or the increase in the intensity of the tests, I am uncertain. Not that it matters but I can finally feel my body wearing out. It won't be long before they push me too far.

After yet another grueling day of tests, one of the scientists approaches me, a grim look on his face. "This will be the final test and as such, will most likely be the most painful one you've experienced," he says, placing his hand gently on my bruised arm. I ignore him, staring out the darkening window above me, refusing to give him the satisfaction of a response. I should feel a sense of relief that the pain will end, but I don't. I deserve every ounce of pain they have inflicted on me and then some. Nothing I do could ever pay back what I have done to my family, and I hope that this test is everything his tone promised. I am ready to die, ready to be done with the feelings that are doing to my insides what the scientists have done to the rest of me. I don't know if there is life after death, but I am ready to find out.

Several scientists surround me in a frenzy of movement. I am prepped with the wires, double the number that they had initially hooked me up with the first time, and with a sterilizing cloth for the needles. A shudder runs through me as they inject the cold fluid into both of my arms and finally my neck. The prick of the needle there feels like a jolt of lightning flowing through all of my extremities, making me jump. As the fluid begins warming up inside me, they push the button, turning the power on to the wires. Searing pain, unlike anything I have experienced in this room so far, rips through every inch of my body. A single tear escapes the corner of my eye, rolling down my face as I watch the full moon rise into my view out the window above.

IN CONCLUSION
Reflection by John Graham

The book you are holding right now has truly been a labor of love for me. As an author, I have always imagined different stories and thought to myself what a wonderful book they would make, but unfortunately, like most creative people in the world, I've come to realize that there never seems to be enough time in the day to juggle work, family, and creative ventures.

When I thought of the concept of Nation of the Moon years ago, I sat down and wrote up an outline for a book that would never be completed. Even though I loved the idea, I knew the moment I clicked "save" on my computer, that I would never have the time to sit down and write out a novel. So it sat on my hard drive as I chased my other creative ventures.

In early 2015, it struck me that I could use my stories and experience to help new creators even more. I took my idea for Nation of the Moon and put it out into the creative community, asking for unpublished authors who might want to write a short story based in this world. This would allow me to get new authors some visibility, while also giving me a chance to learn more about the anthology book arena. I received interest from authors and things started rolling along. I greatly admire the authors in this book for their ability to craft a story with minimal information to go on. My goal was to not explain every detail of the event and leave much of what happened to speculation, just like what would happen in real life. I wanted to leave some of the mystery, so I asked everyone to end their stories at the rise of the following full moon or before.

Then, in 2021, I asked for more submissions and received more stories to make this book even bigger and better. My goal will be to continue growing this world over the years to come, so stay tuned.

I hope you enjoyed the book you've just read and appreciate the fact that you have helped bring a new group of authors into the spotlight. If you are a new author and find yourself to be inspired by the stories in this book and decide you want to write your own Nation of the Moon story, then go ahead. After you finish, reach out to me with your work to be featured in a future edition of the book.

Much thanks.

John Graham

October 2021

FIGID Press

MEET THE AUTHORS

Jonathan byrd

A Maryland-born sci-fi enthusiast, Jonathan Lee Byrd is a creative human with an old soul and a keen eye for art. He has dabbled in just about every art form as he seeks a comfortable outlet for his love of creating. Several of his short stories can be found on Thought Catalog, and he currently records experimental surf rock in the band ghost reef. Jonathan lives with his wife, writer and comedian Simone Le Ann, in Maryland with their three sons, dog, and cat.

Johnny craft

Johnny Craft is a writer, husband, and father (not in that order). He loves comics, horror, and writing any genre with a comedic twist. His ultimate writing goal is to work for DC Comics and to write a feature film adaptation of Webster's Dictionary.
Find him on Twitter and Instagram at CRAFTSCAPECOMIX

Aaron Farrow

Aaron Farrow is a hobby writer and self-described geek/horror aficionado. His work in this book is his first published short story. His only other piece of published work is in FIGID Press' "Survivor's Zombinac".

Cody Grady

Cody lives in Indianapolis with his family and is an obsessive hobbyist. Their home is crowded with his projects that never seem to get finished. Most days Cody finds himself contemplating the inevitable downfall of modern society, half hoping Cthulhu will gobble us all up instead. He is proud to publish his first work in the Nation of the Moon anthology and also help with the editing process.

John Graham

John is a father, writer, creator, and publisher living in Brownsburg, Indiana. His passion is creating things and often describes himself has having "Creativity ADHD" because he constantly shifts from project to project. John loves helping new creators and is always willing to help at FIGIDPress@Gmail.com.

Patrick Handlon

Often described as one of the most impactful pop-culture humor writers of our time, Patrick has branched out into short story writing for this anthology edition. You can find more information about Patrick's work at www.DEADCATCOMIX.com.

Matthew Heslop

Matt lives in Utah and is a father of two. He's a proud owner of the Green Bay Packers and a patriot. Over the years he has worked as a Salt Lake City Police Officer and served in the Air Force during Operation Iraqi Freedom. Currently, he finds himself looking down the barrel of his fifties, which are approaching quickly.

Casey Little

Casey grew up in a small house out in the country with her parents and older brother. She has learned to enjoy the simple things in life and some of her hobbies include fishing and volunteering. She also loves writing and illustrating her own works.

Christopher Moshier

Christopher Moshier is the owner of My Media Helper, Inc. and a System Administrator at the United States Department of Veterans Affairs, focusing primarily on their Intranet Services. His writing consists of several comic books, an online comedy series called "The Church," the Novel Morgana X, and many other things in-between.

At the time of him writing this biography in the third person for this anthology you are now reading, he's editing a novel that incorporates his experiences about the crazy world of online dating while recovering from alcoholism. It's a train wreck you can only possibly imagine.

Feel free to reach out to him at contact@mymediahelper.com

E.M. Nelson

E.M. Nelson is an aspiring, up and coming author currently working on her own novel series. Her piece in this book is her debut into the writing world. When she's not busy writing, she enjoys long afternoon naps and walks, if her six children allow her that is.

Marie Newbold

Marie Newbold has been escaping into books since she could walk. Raised by a wise mother on the classics of science fiction and fantasy, none of her daydreams involved her own backyard – unless dragons or spaceships were picking her up from it.

Thirty years later, Marie has raised the pen in an attempt to pass forward the gift of a good story. In between boy wrangling, dog soothing, and a desk job involving too many numbers, Marie is forming her own worlds for lonely girls and boys to find their salvation from boredom. Visit her at newboldarts.com to see where her daydreams have taken her lately.

figid press

Finally I Got it Done!

Contact: John Graham at FIGIDPress@Gmail.com

Made in the USA
Monee, IL
10 November 2021